"I'm sorry th
embarrassin

"I didn't say I was
"Who posted the photos?"

Who had been close enough to them to overhear their conversation that night by the fire? Everyone had been milling around. But Lila hadn't seen anyone taking photos.

Although she'd been a bit preoccupied. A herd of dancing reindeer could've traipsed through the cobblestone terrace, and she probably wouldn't have noticed. Such was the continuing Sam effect on her sensibilities.

She shrugged. "I don't know who originally posted the pictures. AnnaBeth's mother sent them to her. Apparently, she knows Mrs. Lindstrom."

"Mrs. Lindstrom posted the photos?"

"I'm not sure. The photos have gone viral."

He flinched. She tried not to wince at his reaction. This was awful. Simply awful.

"It doesn't matter now who posted them." He crossed his arms. "What matters is where we go from here."

Miserable, she nodded. "I'll tell everyone there's been a misunderstanding."

"Hang on." He took hold of her arm. "Let's think about this first. What if we *were* engaged…?"

Lisa Carter and her family make their home in North Carolina. In addition to her Love Inspired novels, she writes romantic suspense for Abingdon Press. When she isn't writing, Lisa enjoys traveling to romantic locales, teaching writing workshops and researching her next exotic adventure. She has strong opinions on barbecue and ACC basketball. She loves to hear from readers. Connect with Lisa at lisacarterauthor.com.

Books by Lisa Carter

Love Inspired

Visit the Author Profile page at Harlequin.com.

The Christmas Bargain

Lisa Carter

LOVE INSPIRED
INSPIRATIONAL ROMANCE

LOVE INSPIRED®
INSPIRATIONAL ROMANCE

Recycling programs
for this product may
not exist in your area.

ISBN-13: 978-1-335-55399-7

The Christmas Bargain

Copyright © 2020 by Lisa Carter

All rights reserved. No part of this book may be used or reproduced in
any manner whatsoever without written permission except in the case of
brief quotations embodied in critical articles and reviews.

This is a work of fiction. Names, characters, places and incidents are either the
product of the author's imagination or are used fictitiously. Any resemblance
to actual persons, living or dead, businesses, companies, events or locales is
entirely coincidental.

This edition published by arrangement with Harlequin Books S.A.

For questions and comments about the quality of this book,
please contact us at CustomerService@Harlequin.com.

Love Inspired
22 Adelaide St. West, 40th Floor
Toronto, Ontario M5H 4E3, Canada
www.Harlequin.com

Printed in U.S.A.

And God saw every thing that he had made,
and, behold, it was very good.
—*Genesis* 1:31

Chapter One

Whoever was making that terrible racket needed to stop.

Rolling over in bed, Lila Penry buried her head underneath the pillow.

Thumps followed. Metal screeched. She groaned.

Where was that banging coming from? And why now, at the insanely early hour of—she squinted at the digital clock beside her bed— eight in the morning?

Bleary-eyed, she raised her head. "It's late-start Friday," she muttered to the drawn blinds in her bedroom. She had no classes to teach until this afternoon.

Due to her impending plus-one wedding crisis, she'd spent half the night perusing an online dating site. Agonizing for hours as she crafted a profile. Yet with her finger poised over the keypad, she'd lost her nerve and deleted it.

Something rattled. A clang resounded. Followed by a clatter.

A thundering crash jolted her out of bed.

"For the love of Monet," she shouted to no one in particular.

Last night at dinner, Dad told her he'd hired someone to paint her house. But this…this over-eagerness was ridiculous. It sounded like they were ripping apart the house Granny had left to her. Overhead, feet clomped across the roof.

Teeth gnashing, she raced downstairs. Spotting a ladder and a pair of blue jean-clad legs through the picture window in the living room, she unlocked the bolt and barreled outside. Her bare feet smacked across the gray-planked porch.

"What are you doing?" she yelled at the blue jeans. "Stop!"

The hammering ceased. Rung by rung, tan work boots descended. Foot by booted foot.

Revealing a long-sleeved gray Henley… A well-muscled chest…broad shoulders and finally… Sam.

First she went hot, then cold from sheer mortification.

Whenever she wasn't around him, she believed she must misremember how absurdly handsome Sam Gibson was.

Then one glance—like now—and she knew she hadn't come close to the physical perfection of the man standing beside the ladder.

As always, at the sight of him, her heart sped up a little.

Over six feet, he was tall compared to her five-foot-five stature. The former high school quarterback's dark blond curls were still tousled. But the cleft in his chin was hidden by the beard scruff he'd worn since returning to North Carolina after a stint in the Navy.

"Lila."

And the only reason he knew her name?

Truelove was a small town. They'd been in the same class from kindergarten through high school. Although he'd been the most popular and eligible guy on campus, Sam had been unfailingly nice to everyone.

Including klutzy, socially awkward, late bloomer, braces-wearing, frizzy-haired Lila. She'd long since grown out of the braces. The hair, however…

Her hair remained the bane of her existence.

As he stepped onto the ground, his to-die-for eyes crinkled. "What're you doing here?"

Too late, she became aware of the bronze Chevy pickup with the Paint by the Numbers logo emblazoned on the side.

In the early-morning November chill, her

breath fogged. "I—I…" Desperately, she finger-combed bed hair out of her face. "I live here."

Those eyes of his followed the movement of her hand. And she became aware of an even more horrendous truth.

Part of her nightly routine was to pineapple her impossibly curly hair on top of her head before she went to bed. And despite her special satin pillowcase, after tossing and turning most of the night, her hair probably looked like a squirrel had nested there.

Of all the people in the whole wide world—

"Aren't you cold?" His gaze traveled from the top of her head to her feet and to her face.

"Y-yes," she rasped.

Gathering the tattered remnants of her dignity, she wrapped her arms around herself. She shifted from one foot to the other, the wooden boards cold against the soles of her feet.

Without a speck of makeup on her face, she was standing on her front steps in her favorite comfy flannel pajamas. The ones with cats all over them. Christmas cats.

From the bemused look on his devastatingly handsome features, he probably viewed her as one of those pathetic cat ladies. And was pondering how many felines were going to pour out of the open door behind her.

Would the embarrassment never end?

Sam stuck the claw of the hammer in the front pocket of his jeans. "Didn't your dad tell you I was coming?"

Her father had said a painter was coming. Leaving out one small but all-important detail—that the painter was Sam Gibson.

What was it with men?

They were useless as fonts of information. Did men not talk while they golfed or met for lunch? Did they not talk while at the store or work? Did they not talk, period?

"I'm sorry." Sam rested his hand on the ladder. "I didn't realize anyone lived here. I guess I woke you up."

Her cheeks felt hot. As hot as the color of a poinsettia. Color was her life. But the upside to resembling a poinsettia? Perhaps her face no longer resembled the walking dead.

She pushed several strands of hair out of her face. Although in the circumstances, if now wasn't the time to hide behind the bane of her existence, she didn't know what would qualify.

"I promised your dad I'd start today. And when I heard on the radio this morning there's a snowstorm in the Sierra Nevada—"

"Why the Sierra Nevada?"

He blinked at her for a moment. And if she hadn't known him her entire life—in an abstract,

on the outside, plain girl, groupie kind of way—
she would've believed he looked unsure of himself.

Lunacy, of course. Because she was so inca-
pable of making the usually glib, supremely self-
confident football hero feel anything.

"Th-the storm is predicted to make its way
across the Midwest over the course of the week."
He cleared his throat. "Which means once the
storm crosses the Appalachian Mountains, Truelove's forecast changes, too." He crossed his arms
over his chest. Muscles rippled and bunched.

Her turn to blink.

"I've only got this week to pressure wash,
make repairs, caulk, tape and paint the house
before the temperature drops."

"Oh." For want of somewhere safer to land
her gaze, she flicked her eyes toward the roof. "I
just imagined painting to be a quieter activity."

"It's nothing like the incredible landscapes you
paint, but painting a house does have its more
contemplative moments."

Her eyes cut to him. A smile curved the corners of his ruggedly attractive mouth.

She swallowed. "You've seen my work?"

"I saw the chalk painting you did on the sidewalk in front of our rival's school. And the mural
you painted in the arts wing senior year."

High school had been a sort of social apart-
heid for her. Yet during her junior year, when

her childhood friend Paige and her cheerleader cohorts begged Lila to lend her talents to Spirit Week, she'd been flattered. The first and only time the popular girls included her. Homecoming weekend, they'd sneaked over there in the dark of night. She'd been terrified of being caught, but exhilarated.

"The mural's still there, you know."

She did know. She and the art teacher who'd inspired her to pursue her dreams got together once in a while for coffee.

"The reason it's so noisy is that I'm removing the gutters, but I should be done later today. The rest of my crew are finishing another job but will be here later to help." Lifting his navy-blue ball cap—the name of a USS destroyer embroidered on the brim—he resettled the cap atop his mop of tousled curls. "Is that okay?"

Hands warming in her arms, her fingers curled in appreciation. "Sure. I'll try to stay out of your way."

Sam cocked his head. "You won't be in my way."

In unaccustomed proximity to her unrequited schoolgirl crush, she quivered. He had a debilitating effect on her nerve endings. "Wh-where's Emma Cate?"

At the mention of the little girl, his face transformed. "Since it's late-start Friday for preschoolers, too, my mom's keeping her this morning."

Two years ago when his sister and brother-in-law unexpectedly died, he'd taken Emma Cate to raise as his own without hesitation. And though he was only twenty-six, he was a good dad.

She shivered again.

He braced his hands on the ladder to climb up again. "You should go inside and get warm."

She should, but it was so much nicer talking with him. "You're blessed to have Emma Cate."

"Having her in my life is the most wonderful thing that ever happened to me." He flashed her a smile.

Strong, even, white teeth.

A knee-buckling, ridiculously stomach-quivering smile. She felt quite faint. Yet while she would love nothing more than to stand around and stare at Sam Gibson all day, she did have other places to be.

Since her day had gotten an *early* start, she might as well run some errands before she met her friend AnnaBeth at the Mason Jar Diner. With effort, she unglued her feet from the floor. And closed her mouth.

Drooling was unattractive on a grown woman.

For fear of further disgracing herself, she fluttered her fingers at him and fled inside to the safety of her house.

But if her plans went forward as she hoped, by the new year, she'd be the new artist in residence in sunny California. Snow and Sam Gibson would be the stuff of distant memory.

An hour later, while perched on the ladder again, Sam watched Lila pull out of the driveway and head toward downtown.

The majority of the houses on the street were built at the turn of the last century. Located in one of the small town's older neighborhoods, Lila's two-story Arts and Crafts bungalow with the broad-planked porch sat adjacent to IdaLee Moore's gingerbread Victorian. At the thought of Miss IdaLee, he grimaced.

Married, divorced or spinster, "Miss" was an honorary title of respect bestowed on any southern lady who was your elder. No matter if the Miss was elderly or not.

Lila's great-aunt IdaLee and her matchmaking double-name cronies were determined to help everyone in the Blue Ridge mountain town find their happily-ever-after. Whether the recipients of their efforts wanted them to or not.

In his case, definitely not.

A few hours after his unexpected encounter with Lila, Sam got in his truck to head to the elementary school. He and Emma Cate had a standing lunch date for late-start Fridays. Once his crew arrived this afternoon, they'd make short work of removing Lila's remaining gutters.

He found his niece waiting for him outside the cafeteria. Seeing him, she immediately disengaged from the rest of her classmates standing in line and hurled herself at him.

Emma Cate's arms went around his legs. "Daddy Sam!"

Lips curving, he rested his palm on her silky blond head. "Hey, baby doll."

Her teacher caught his eye and gestured to the wall plastered with art. "Get Emma Cate to show you her drawings before you eat lunch." She herded her charges into the cafeteria.

Emma Cate's little hand tucked into his, he stepped closer to examine the various renderings.

"Which one is your favorite, Daddy Sam?"

"The pictures drawn by Emma Cate are my favorite."

She shook her head, setting her pale blond braids in motion. "Which one do you like the best?"

He scanned the drawings taped to the wall. "This one is nice." He motioned to her amazingly lifelike depiction of a horse.

She'd seen the horse a few weeks ago when her class took an excursion to the FieldStone Dude Ranch. And judging from the other childlike illustrations, he might be biased, but he believed she possessed art skills far in advance of the other four-year-olds.

He tapped his finger to the tip of her nose. "We better go inside and eat before lunch is over."

Squeezing his hand, she pulled him into the cafeteria. "First, we got to get de tray, Daddy Sam."

They'd done lunch every Friday since she went to school in September. But he allowed the little girl to take him through the now-familiar ritual of cafeteria protocol. Plucking utensils from the plastic caddy. Yanking napkins out of the holder. Sliding the tray along the metal rails.

She ordered for them both. Always the same— a slice of cheese pizza, a cup of steamed broccoli (his compromise to the pizza) and a small carton of milk.

Leaving the lunch lady at the register, he carried the tray to the table where Emma Cate directed him. After he plopped down on the small stool, the little girl regaled him with her morning adventures since he'd seen her last. About four hours ago.

She talked. He listened. He let her do most of the eating.

Not old enough for kindergarten, she was enrolled in the Head Start program at the elementary school. Juggling single parenting and starting his paint contracting business, the program was a godsend for him.

But that first day, going into the school building, she'd seemed so small. Leaving her in the classroom had been one of the hardest things he'd ever done.

Hard for him, but not for her. She loved going to school with her friends. And he was glad she was happy.

Yet the program was designed for disadvantaged children. When he was a boy, he and his sister had practically been the poster children for at-risk families. Now he was determined to make his business a success.

With a con man and swindler for a father, he was out to remake the Gibson name into something Emma Cate could be proud to claim. He would do everything in his power to reverse the bitter Gibson legacy he'd inherited and ensure she had a loving, stable life, full of opportunities.

His cell pinged. He fished it out of his jeans and read the text from Lila's father, requesting a meeting. Forehead creased, he typed a response. He hoped Mr. Penry wasn't unhappy with the work he'd done so far. He needed this job.

"Looks like I have to go, baby doll."

A line etched the space between her perfect little brows. "But I didn't show you my favorite picture, Daddy Sam."

He glanced at his watch. Ten minutes were left in her lunch period. If he hurried, he'd still have plenty of time to meet Cliff Penry. "Let's do it now."

They quickly deposited their trash into the proper receptacles.

In the hallway once more, she drew his attention to another of her sketches. "Dis one's my favorite, Daddy Sam."

Recognizing the image of their humble mobile home, his heart sank. He wanted so much more than he could provide for her in their present circumstances. But he'd put in a bid to paint a high-end phased development in nearby Asheville last week. The contract would give his crew steady work for the next three years. And he could look for a better place to live.

"Dat's you." In an effort to be helpful, she pointed to the tallest figure in the drawing. "Dere's me and dere's…"

He squinted at the medium-height figure. Shoulder-length red curls. Big gray-blue eyes. The woman had to be—

"—Miss Penry." Emma Cate smiled.

Art was her favorite subject. Other than Sam and her grandparents, art teacher Miss Lila Penry was her favorite person.

Each night, Emma Cate gave him a blow-by-blow account of what the delightfully fabulous

Miss Penry had worn that day. The child was a big fan of the art teacher's accessories. Apparently, Lila Penry had as many scarves as there were days in the year.

He reckoned he knew as much about Lila's wardrobe as she did. But he appreciated the interest she'd taken in his niece. He'd known her since they were both Emma Cate's age.

A free spirit with her fluttery skirts and hand-crafted jewelry, she'd marched to the beat of a different drummer. Her head always in the clouds, Lila hadn't been like the other teenage girls. Quirky and slightly eccentric, she hadn't gotten involved in the usual high school drama.

Even then, he'd recognized she was wildly talented. Unlike him, she was also comfortable in her own skin, and he admired that about her. Her silvery eyes had often held a faraway look. As if imagining more exciting worlds.

Living with the shame of his father's misdeeds and grappling with his mother's illness, a world which he wouldn't have minded escaping to. Perhaps that was why he'd joined the US Navy after graduation.

A bell rang.

Sam kissed his niece's sweet little hand. "Lunch is over."

Her teacher gathered the students together. At the end of the line, he and Emma Cate trooped down the hall with the others. Outside their classroom, the teacher directed the children to go inside and take their seats.

Sam turned to leave. "I'll see you after work."

Her hold tightened on his hand.

"Your teacher's waiting, baby doll." He frowned. "I've got an appointment."

Her lower lip wobbled.

Sam crouched beside her. "What's wrong?"

Her blue eyes welled. "I—I miss you when I'm at school." She threw her arms around his neck.

Gut clenching, he rocked onto his heels. Before-and after-school care made for a long day for a four-year-old.

She didn't remember her mom or dad. He was the only parent she'd ever truly known. He loved her so much. He was all she had. He was her world. A privilege and responsibility he didn't take lightly.

The love went both ways. She was all he had. She was his world, too. But he had to work. He had bills to pay.

He tried prying her stranglehold from around his neck. "Emma—"

"She loves when you visit her at school." A gnarled, blue-veined hand rested lightly on Emma Cate's blond locks. "Don't you, sweetheart?"

He looked up, and it was enough to cause the child to loosen her grip.

The oldest of the Double Name Club members, Miss IdaLee had taught generations of Truelove students. Himself included. He'd forgotten the diminutive, retired schoolteacher volunteered with the Head Start program in the afternoons.

Snow-white hair in a bun atop her head, Ida-Lee held out her hand to his little girl. Her violet-blue eyes twinkled. "It's Isaiah Abernathy's turn for show-and-tell. And whatever he brought in the box barks."

Emma Cate let go of him. "Is—is it a puppy?" she breathed.

The prim Miss IdaLee winked at him. "Isaiah says everyone will get a chance to pet his new dog."

Bouncing on her toes, she clasped her hands under her chin. "Oh. Oh. Oh."

"Does that sound like something you'd be interested in doing? Petting a puppy?"

"'Bye, Daddy Sam." She threw him a kiss. "See ya later." She dashed inside the classroom.

"I guess I know where I stand." He ran his hand over his head. "Replaced already."

"Better a puppy than a boy." IdaLee smiled. "But they'll be next."

"Don't remind me," he groaned. "Definitely not looking forward to that."

She patted his sleeve. "You're a good dad."

"Thank you, Miss IdaLee. I try."

"How about trying harder to give that little girl a mommy?" The old woman tilted her head. "How'd your date go with the new lady at the bank last weekend?"

Should've seen that one coming.

Any conversation with one of the matchmakers was fraught with potential matrimonial landmines. Since returning to his hometown, the old ladies had taken one look at his motherless niece and made it their personal mission to find his happily-ever-after. Forces of nature, the matchmakers didn't take no for an answer.

They'd ganged up on him. Caught him in a weak moment. Hounded him near to death. Until finally he'd agreed to a blind date with the woman who worked at the ice cream shop.

Followed by a date with the waitress at the Mason Jar. And then there'd been the nurse at the hospital. One awkward date after the other. Nice women, but he didn't have the time or the heart for dating.

IdaLee folded her arms. "Are you free Saturday night? I've found the perfect girl for you."

"That's what you said the last time." He scraped his hand over his face, wondering how to dodge this latest bullet. "And the time before that."

"I never said the others were perfect." Her thin shoulders rose and fell. "But they served their purpose. Part of the recalibration process. I've made the necessary adjustments now."

Snared in the crosshairs of matchmaking mayhem, he gulped. Who would it be this time? The petite blonde at the grocery store? The brunette at the home-improvement store?

He edged away. "I have a business to run and a child to raise."

With little time or energy in his life for anything else. Which was fine with him. More than fine.

Except when he ran into old high school buddies around town with their wives and families. And he remembered the lonely hours after Emma Cate went to bed every night.

"Don't worry." She wagged her bony finger. "We've got your best interests at heart."

Maybe so, but he couldn't help but wonder how much their best was going to hurt.

"I know trust doesn't come easy, Samuel. But you're in good hands with the Double Name Club." She opened her palms as if to demonstrate. "We'll have you sorted by Christmas."

There were so many things wrong with what she'd said, his brain didn't know where to land first.

By Christmas? His love life—or lack thereof—

in the hands of the matchmakers? Both ideas filled him with no small amount of horror. Time to make his escape.

"Uh, excuse me, Miss IdaLee." He backpedaled. "I've got to get back to a job."

Turning on his heel, he practically sprinted out of the building. Only when he reached his truck in the school parking lot did he take an easy breath. That had been a close call.

Working on the Penry house, he'd have to take extra pains to avoid any more interactions with her next-door neighbor, Miss IdaLee. Because if she had her way, quicker than he could say, "Merry Christmas," she and her sidekicks would have him painted into a corner.

A matrimonial corner.

Chapter Two

Lila parked in the school parking lot just off the village square. After lunch, she had a few art classes to teach this afternoon. She got out of her car.

With a determined effort, she pushed aside the memory of her earlier funny-strange encounter with Sam Gibson. A delicious blast of apple-crisp air flicked across her skin. She lifted her face to the sunny late-November sky.

The weather had been unseasonably warm. The pungent aroma of burning leaves wafted past her nostrils. But once the expected storm worsened the weather, a glorious day such as this would only be a fond recollection.

Her last Blue Ridge autumn. Or at least, her last for a while. And for once, the idea of leaving didn't sit as well with her as she'd imagined.

It would be Thanksgiving soon. And after that,

the small town in the Blue Ridge Mountains of North Carolina would be decked out in holiday splendor. She loved Christmas.

Clutching the strap of her tote bag, she hurried across the village green and past the deserted gazebo to the Mason Jar Diner. The popular local hangout appeared packed. And she was running late to meet AnnaBeth for lunch.

Even though she had a Master's in Fine Arts, jobs weren't plentiful for a landscape artist like herself. Her parents were good but unimaginative people. They'd never understood her creative energy and hadn't been enthusiastic about her career choice. As a compromise, she'd double majored. Getting her teaching certificate had proven a wise decision.

But with the current emphasis on math and science, the arts curriculum had been slashed in most schools. She was fortunate to have been hired as the part-time art teacher at Truelove Elementary. At the small mountain school, her schedule was flexible, leaving her plenty of time to teach art classes at the rec center, too. She also sold her paintings in local galleries and did work on commission.

She yanked open the door of the diner, and the bell jangled over her head. The yeasty aroma of biscuits floated past her nostrils. Her belly rumbled. Waitresses bustled between the kitchen and dining room carrying loaded trays.

At the sight of two members of the Double Name Club—more notoriously known as the Truelove Matchmakers—she stuttered to a stop. The elderly women, GeorgeAnne Allen and ErmaJean Hicks, occupied their favorite table underneath the community bulletin board. No sign of her great-aunt IdaLee.

The ladies were infamous for poking their powdered noses where they didn't belong. They took the town motto—Truelove, Where True Love Awaits—a little too seriously.

Not that she'd ever found herself a target of their machinations. The old women probably didn't know what to do with her any more than her parents did. As a kid, she'd once overhead Aunt IdaLee telling her mother how different she was from the other girls.

In that regard, not much had changed. Except she wasn't a little girl any more.

She spotted AnnaBeth. The vivacious redhead waved Lila over to one of the booths. As she wove her way among the tables, various people called out friendly greetings. People she'd known her entire life.

One of the many reasons she couldn't wait to bid her hometown farewell for good.

Lila was so ready for the next chapter of her

life. A chance to reinvent herself. To redefine herself on her own terms. To break away from everyone's image of Cliff and Myra's never-fits-in, artsy daughter.

"Sorry I'm late." She slipped into the booth. "How did you manage to score a table?"

"I got here early to beat the rush." Married not quite a year, AnnaBeth's green eyes sparkled. "I went ahead and ordered your usual."

Money was tight on an artist's income, but the weekly lunch with her cousin Jonas's new wife was one of her few treats.

"Thanks." Ducking out from under her purse strap, she laid the bag beside her on the seat. "I got out of bed pretty early for a late-start Friday." She propped her arms on the sticky laminate tabletop. "But I ran errands, and the time got away from me."

A social media influencer on the successful blog *Heart's Home*, AnnaBeth Stone was the most stylish person Lila knew. She'd been a welcome addition to their family. A kindred spirit.

The waitress dropped off their order.

"What has my son done in art class lately?"

Every week, AnnaBeth asked the same question. She didn't mind keeping her friend updated.

"With Thanksgiving on the horizon, the kindergarten class is working on a project about what they're thankful for." Lila smiled. "Hunter is very thankful for his new mommy."

Happiness glowed from AnnaBeth's face. "His new mommy is very thankful for him." This would be their first official Christmas as a family.

Last year, the sweet little cowboy had wished for a mommy for Christmas. AnnaBeth wasn't originally from Truelove, but driving through a holiday snowstorm, she'd become stranded there. Despite coming from a wealthy background, she'd managed to fit seamlessly into the life of the tiny hamlet. And into rancher Jonas's heart.

For a split second, something stirred in Lila's heart. The desire to be loved like her dear friend. The longing to love someone in return. The yearning for a family and home of her own.

She shook her head. Maybe someday. For now, her focus was on furthering her art career.

"What's wrong?"

"Nothing." Lila shrugged. "Just thinking about California."

"I don't understand why you're in such a rush to leave Truelove." AnnaBeth folded her napkin in her lap. "You enjoy teaching art to the kids."

She bit the end of her French fry. "I do enjoy the fresh, out-of-the-box way they view the world—it inspires me. But as an artist I need to continue to challenge myself."

Unlike her more ginger locks, AnnaBeth's hair was a glorious shade of red.

"Have you heard anything about your grant application?"

Lila fiddled with a sugar packet. "Not yet, but it's early days. They'll award the artist-in-residence position in mid-December."

AnnaBeth took a sip of water. "I know you'll get it."

Lila glanced out the plate-glass window overlooking Main Street and the town square. "A small-town girl doesn't have much going for her in comparison to the other candidates."

She'd entered her portfolio in a juried art competition. She was saving every dime, so if she received the grant, she could leave her hometown behind for the big city and afford the higher cost of living. She wanted to take her art to the next level.

The grant was the first step on the journey—her personal metamorphosis—to becoming the Lila Penry she wanted to be.

A world-renowned artist. Surrounded by people who got her. Who understood her. She was looking for her tribe. And she definitely wouldn't find her tribe in sleepy, little Truelove.

"So what have you decided to do about that other thing?"

Lila dipped a fry into her vanilla milkshake. "What other thing?"

"Not so much a what as a who." AnnaBeth pushed her plate away. "Who are you going to bring as your plus-one to the wedding at the resort?"

"Keep your voice down," she hissed.

She cut her eyes at the matchmakers standing at the cash register. Neither of her great-aunt's compatriots in mischief turned around, but the old women had ears like bats.

AnnaBeth rolled her eyes. "Seriously, Lila?"

She hunched forward over the table. "Intelligence agencies around the world could learn a thing or two from the Truelove grapevine."

The bell jangled, announcing the duo's exit.

"Why did you RSVP for a plus-one if you didn't have anyone to go to the wedding with you?"

"Temporary insanity." Lila cradled her head in her hands. "At the time, I was under the influence of an empty carton of fudge ripple ice cream."

AnnaBeth laughed. Lila didn't. This was what she got for scrolling through Paige Lindstrom's engagement photos on social media. And for throwing herself a pity party.

"But you and Paige are lifelong friends." AnnaBeth steepled her hands. "You're her maid of honor. Will it really matter so much if you arrive for the wedding weekend without a date?"

"Since my college friends will be there? Since Tristan was my boyfriend first? And I introduced the two of them? Yes." She sighed. "Yes, it does."

AnnaBeth winced. "I didn't realize the backstory involved."

She bit her lip. "It's complicated."

Embarrassing and humiliating, too.

AnnaBeth perked. "You could borrow Jonas."

"Don't think I haven't considered it, but I don't think that will work." She slumped. "Too many people will be there who know we're related."

AnnaBeth opened her hands. "What will you do?"

The wedding was only three weeks away. Panic burbled inside her chest. She had to think of something fast.

Sam pulled away from the school. Rounding the square, he headed down Main. Veering off, he turned into the Penry neighborhood and eased the truck to a stop beside the curb. His crew hadn't yet arrived.

In the driveway, a distinguished-looking man in his midfifties got out of a sedan and waved him over. Switching off the ignition, Sam stepped out of the truck.

Cliff Penry held out his hand. "Thanks for

meeting me on such short notice. I wanted to talk face-to-face with you about a few questions regarding the contract."

His stomach tanking, Sam shook the CPA's hand.

Yesterday while Emma Cate was at school, Mr. Penry had contacted him and asked for an estimate. Using his giant tape measure, Sam had walked around the perimeter of the house to determine the square footage. That afternoon, he'd sent his estimate via email. Penry had responded almost immediately with the go-ahead.

The knot tightened in his stomach. "Is there a problem, Mr. Penry?"

"No problem. I wanted you to take me through the repairs you'll need to make before painting." Lila's father walked with him over to the house. "Jonas Stone had nothing but great things to say about the work your crew did at the ranch over the summer."

"That's good to hear, sir."

Word of mouth about the quality of his work was essential.

"This was your mother's house, right?" He got out a pencil and pad to take notes. "I was sorry to hear of her death."

Back in the spring, old Mrs. Penry passed away in her sleep.

Cliff Penry nodded. "We miss her, but she

lived a good, long life and is enjoying her reward."

"The soffit will need replacing." He pointed
toward the eave over the garage. "The bottom of
the door has also rotted."

Penry squatted by the door. "Appears so."
Hands on his knees, he pushed upright. "I grew
up in this house. My mother did, too. With the
estate settled, my wife and I would like to see it
restored to its original glory."

Old Mrs. Penry had been a sweet woman. The
grandmother of Emma Cate's beloved art teacher,
Lila. After growing up in one rented trailer after
the other, he could only imagine what it would've
been like to have a family home place like this.
But maybe one day if he worked hard enough,
his niece would.

He drew Mr. Penry's attention to another half
dozen repairs that would need to be made before
the painting could commence.

"And I have another question." Penry scratched
his head. "About the gutters…"

Sweat broke out on his forehead. Had Lila
complained to her father about the noise? That
didn't correspond with what he remembered of
her character, but what did he know?

Until this morning, he hadn't really talked to
her since high school.

"I have to remove the gutters before my crew

can begin painting." He stuffed the pad and pencil in his pocket. "The gutters aren't in bad shape, though. If we install a leaf guard to help with drainage, you'll be fine."

Penry arched his eyebrow. "So you believe there's no need for brand-new gutters?"

What was the CPA hoping to hear? That Sam could save him a ton of money? Or would he view his suggestion as proof of sloppy, corner-cutting measures?

He squared his jaw. He could only give his honest opinion. If Penry wanted to throw good money at unnecessary expenses, Sam reckoned that was his business.

"Looks like the gutters were installed a few years ago. Unless you've noticed problems, I think you're fine with what you already have, sir."

The CPA's thin mouth twitched. "Good to know." He pushed his black-framed glasses higher onto the bridge of his nose. "How will the cold front affect your timeline?"

He lifted his ball cap and resettled it on his head. "My crew is finishing Jake McAbee's house at Apple Valley Orchard today. And then we're putting all our time onto your project. We'll get it done before the bad weather arrives. Will that work for you?"

"Works great for me."

Relief whooshed through him. *Thank You, God.* Jake's house had been the last project on their books. An idle crew meant nobody got paid.

"Thank you, sir."

"One other item to settle." Mr. Penry withdrew a checkbook from the inside pocket of his suit coat. "How much of a deposit do you require?"

He shook his head. "I prefer that my clients don't pay me anything until the job is completed to their satisfaction."

Penry's brows lifted. "I admire your dedication to doing a job well." He eyed Sam a long moment. "In today's world, I don't see that much."

From Sam's perspective, personal integrity was nonnegotiable. And thanks to the lingering bad aftertaste of his deadbeat father, it was an uphill climb for his reputation in the community.

Penry's gaze roamed over the old house. "I can't tell you how wonderful it will be to see this place come alive again."

"If you don't mind me asking, sir. Where did my bid fall in relation to the others?" A delicate question, but it was hard to gauge those things. "High? Low?"

For future reference, he needed to determine how Paint by the Numbers stacked up against the competition.

"You were in the middle. The Goldilocks

zone." A smile warmed Penry's hazel eyes. "Just about right."

Just about right was the opportunity for one last exterior project before the cold set in earnest and they switched to interior painting.

The Penry place would put them in the black this month. And come Christmas, if he was careful, it would also put gifts under the tree for Emma Cate.

Thanks to the Penrys, this might prove a Christmas to remember after all.

Chapter Three

As soon as school let out that afternoon, Lila stopped by the local grocer to buy a few necessities of life. Like chocolate.

Brain food for coming up with an answer to her plus-one problem.

This time of year, once the sun began its descent behind the ridge of the surrounding mountains, darkness fell quickly. When she steered into her driveway, there was no sign of the Paint by the Numbers crew. Or, more importantly, Sam.

But tonight, even the chocolate failed her. She was no closer to a solution when she crawled into bed than she'd been that morning when Mr. Gorgeous woke her out of a sound sleep.

Not that she'd mind if his was the first face she beheld every morning. She rolled her eyes. Like that was ever going to happen.

However, she set her alarm clock to buzz her awake extra early. No need to repeat Friday's fiasco of pineapple hair, no makeup and Christmas-cat jammies. She'd never look like Paige, and therefore never be in Sam's league, but she did have some pride.

She'd just finished a cup of coffee when the sound of slamming doors drew her to the living room window. Twitching aside the curtain, she spotted the white van parked at the curb. Sam's bronze truck pulled alongside.

Three young men piled out of the Paint by the Numbers van. She recognized two of them from high school. Rigo Corrales had been raised in the same trailer park in the hollow across the river as Sam. Lanky Neil McDougall, too.

Sam got out of his truck, and her attention shifted to him. Under the checked flannel shirt, his broad shoulders tapered to a narrow waist. As for his eyes…

A brilliant Dresden blue, his eyes—those fabulous blue orbs of perfection—flicked in her direction.

Blushing furiously, she let the curtain drop. How had he known she was watching? He must think her so stupid.

She headed upstairs to finish getting ready. Her Saturday hair routine took a large part of her morning. It had taken years before she finally learned how to tame her locks. And a lot of hair product experimentation.

It took thirty minutes to damp dry the wet strands with the diffuser. But at last, she shook out her hair in front of the mirror. Voilà.

Soft, frizz-free curls.

Nothing like Paige's glossy, straight-hair standards, but the best Lila could do with what she'd been given.

For a Saturday morning, she dressed with more than her usual care. She emerged from the bathroom in a pair of skinny jeans, a baggy, sage-green sweater and suede ankle boots in a wonderful camel color. She tied a russet-toned scarf into a French knot and let it drape down the front of her sweater.

At the top of the stairs, she hesitated.

She ought to go into her studio and work on the commission for the bank. She bit her lip. She'd much rather… She'd much rather bask in the manly glow that was Sam Gibson. How ridiculous, how over the moon was that?

And yet… She lifted her chin. It wasn't every day good-looking men hung out around her house.

Might as well take advantage of the opportunity. She'd call it art appreciation. Thinking of Sam, she smiled. Art appreciation at its finest.

Creeping into the kitchen, she was startled by

the sound of silence. Two ladders lay propped against the back of the house. She tiptoed into the living room. One ladder rested against the front eaves. But no legs, Sam's or otherwise.

Pulse skittering, she hurried to the front door. Had her hair taken so long they'd gone to lunch already? They wouldn't have walked off without their tools, though, right?

Her heels scudding across the porch, she stumbled out the door and then teetered to an abrupt halt. Munching on ham biscuits, ten pairs of eyes swung in her direction.

Rigo's and the African American man's dark brown eyes. Neil's hazel eyes. Sam's blue-willow-plate eyes. And… She gulped.

Poised to pour the contents of a carafe into Sam's coffee mug, Aunt IdaLee's violet gaze widened.

Brow creasing, Sam got to his feet. The other men rose as well.

"Aunt IdaLee, what are you doing here?"

"They needed a morning snack." Her aunt's bony elbow nudged Sam. "They do better work that way."

Sam scuffed his boot on the step. "Your aunt insisted, and nobody refuses Miss IdaLee."

Lila's great-aunt sniffed. "I should think not."

The African American man extended his

hand. "It's Deon. Deon Scott, Miss Penry." His craggy countenance creased into a smile.

She shook his hand.

IdaLee gestured. "I think you know the rest of these boys."

The "boys" were in their mid-to late twenties.

IdaLee set the carafe onto a step. "Good boys, each and every one. Taught all of them but Deon here when they were knee-high to a grasshopper."

Sam stuffed his hands into his jean pockets. "Deon and I served together in the Navy."

She arched her eyebrow. "This is your paint crew?"

"Yes, ma'am." Rigo grinned. "I supervise the painting." He jabbed his thumb. "Deon oversees the prep work."

Neil brushed his somewhat shaggy auburn hair out of his face. "I'm the grunt worker, but Sam let us buy into the business. Gave us a chance to make a life for our families." He threw her a bashful smile. "My wife and I are expecting our first baby this spring."

She smiled. "Congratulations, Neil."

Even at the best of economic times, jobs were hard to come by in the Appalachians. Neil's father had been an abusive alcoholic. Rigo's family were immigrants. Both men, like Sam, had had a lot of obstacles to overcome.

"And with that lady-killer face of his?" Deon jabbed his thumb. "Gibson woos us the biz."

Sam sputtered. She glanced at him. Surely his good looks weren't news to him?

Neil nodded. "We're partners, you see."

What she saw was that Sam had started a business with honest, decent, hardworking men. Like himself. Giving them an opportunity to make something of themselves. Her admiration for him grew tenfold.

And despite the urging of her common sense, something stirred to life inside her heart.

Soon after, the men returned to work. Lila told them she needed to return to her art. Her aunt returned to her own home next door.

But at regular intervals, Lila peeked out the upstairs window to chart their progress. By lunchtime, yard after yard of white metal gutters lay stacked along the length of the white picket fence.

And somehow she managed to put another layer of detail into the commissioned piece. But she remained uncharacteristically distracted. Detecting the sound of a female voice, she ventured out to the broad expanse of her front porch again.

Only a few feet away across the lawn, Sam and his mother, Kathy Gibson, stood talking together at the top of the stone steps that led down the slight embankment to the street.

Frowning, his gaze flitted to Lila before returning to his mother. "We were getting ready to pressure wash the house."

His mother was a rail-thin, angular woman. The kind the Appalachians had in abundance. It wasn't hard to see where Sam had gotten his looks. Although at fifty-something, her features held only the careworn remnants of a faded rose.

"I don't know what else to do, son. I need the hours, and my manager called. The Christmas retail season has begun." She waved to Lila. "You look pretty as a picture this lovely autumn morning." Her eyes—the same vivid blue as Sam's and Emma Cate's—darted to her son. "Doesn't she?"

Mumbling something, he dropped his gaze to the slate step.

Nothing like putting him on the spot. She felt a tidal wave of crimson blotch her neck. *So... awkward.*

There was a blur of motion. Running up the steps from Mrs. Gibson's sedan, four-year-old Emma Cate whizzed past Sam and her grandmother.

At full throttle, she raced toward Lila. "Miss Penry!"

Her small legs ate up the ground between them. At least one person was glad to see her.

Smiling, she came off the porch to meet her young art student. The little girl threw herself at Lila. Rocking on her heels, her arms went around the child while she fought for equilibrium.

Her uncle hurried forward. "You almost knocked Miss Penry down."

Lifting her head, the adorable little girl let go. Lila immediately missed the warmth of her embrace.

"I sorry, Daddy Sam."

He rubbed his neck. "Don't apologize to me. Apologize to your teacher."

"I sorry, Miss Penry."

Lila fingered the flyaway, smooth-as-silk strand of hair that had come loose from her braid and tucked it behind her petal-shaped ear. "I'm glad to see you, too."

Emma Cate's grandmother joined them.

"Looks like we've got a situation." He scraped his hand over his face. "Mom's been called to work at the outlet mall."

During their high school years, his mother had suffered from a lung ailment. Perhaps the result of working in one of the cotton mills downriver since she was a girl. Before OSHA and the EPA shut them down.

Lila was happy to see a healthy color blooming in his mother's cheeks. "You're looking well, Mrs. Gibson."

His mother extended her hand, showing off a gold wedding band. "It's Mrs. Tate now."

"Congratulations." She hugged Emma Cate's shoulder blades against her legs. "Marriage seems to agree with you."

"It does." His mother smiled and glanced at her granddaughter. "Usually we watch Emma Cate when Sam has a weekend job, but Phil's hauling a big rig across the country." Reaching behind her head, she tightened the band around her blond ponytail. "I'm sorry, son."

"Not your responsibility, Mom. I appreciate everything you and Phil do." He held out his hand to his niece. "We better head home, baby doll." He looked at Lila. "Will it be a problem for the guys to continue without me? They won't finish like I'd hoped but—"

"Why don't you stay and let Emma Cate spend the afternoon with me?"

"Yay!" The little girl fist-pumped the air.

His mother smiled. "How sweet of you to offer."

"I can't impose on you like that." He scowled. "You're working, Lila."

Not so much with the likes of Sam Gibson hanging off the roof of her house, but he didn't need to know that.

And somebody ought to tell him not to frown so much. It would be a shame to spoil such fine looks with deeply grooved lines in that perfect forehead of his.

Not that she'd ever tell him that, of course.

"I'm at a good stopping place for the day." She smiled at Emma Cate and then him. "Please. A girls' afternoon. It'll be fun."

"Puh-leeze. Puh-leeze." A human pogo stick, the child bounced in her pink sneakers. "Puh-leeze, Daddy Sam."

A muscle ticked in his cheek. She could practically see the wheels turning in his head. Hesitation clouded his eyes. Maybe trying to think of a polite way to turn her down without insulting her.

"Something for nothing?" He shook his head. "I can't do that."

A sharp realization pinged inside her chest. He'd probably been the recipient of more than his share of charity as a boy. He was a proud man. He didn't like handouts.

What should I say, Lord? How do I get him to—

"You'd be doing me a favor," she blurted. "That way you can finish power washing my house today and stick to the timeline."

"Then the house would have the rest of the weekend to dry." He gave her a slow nod. "We could keep to the schedule. Start the repairs, caulking and taping bright and early on Monday."

Lila opened her palms. "Exactly."

His mother headed off to work. She and Emma Cate went inside. A gush of water sprayed the back of the house. The water gently rattled against the windowpanes.

Upstairs, she showed the little girl the dormer room under the eaves on the second story that had been hers whenever she visited Granny. Sinking onto the Berber carpet in front of the bookcase, they pulled out Lila's favorite picture books from when she was a child.

They snuggled into the window seat cushion. "Did you know my granny and Miss IdaLee were sisters?" Sam's niece smelled of baby shampoo and soap.

Shaking her head, Emma Cate flipped the page. "I can't read yet, Miss Penry."

Lila smiled. "I'll read, and you enjoy looking at the illustrations."

They didn't get far, however, before the little girl stopped her to ask a question about how the illustrator drew the little boy in the story.

Getting up, she beckoned the child across the hall to her studio. Pulling out a sketchpad, she showed Emma Cate the basics of drawing a human face.

She tilted her head, surveying what she'd drawn. "I'm not very good at creating people."

Her young art protegée motioned toward the half-finished painting on the easel. "But you're very, very good at drawing everything else."

Lila's heart melted. "That may be the nicest thing anyone's ever said to me."

Her work in progress for the bank was a bird's-eye rendering of Truelove at twilight. Like a ribbon, the silvery flash of the river curled in a horseshoe around the town. And beyond the town, she'd captured the smoky indigo smudge of undulating mountain ridges on the horizon. The haze for which the Blue Ridge derived its name.

Emma Cate held the sketchpad out to her.

She shook her head. "It's yours to keep. Fill it with drawings of beautiful things."

Later, they dived into her scarf collection. The little girl's eyes grew wide at the rainbow of glittering, swirling colors.

Pulling a particularly vivid batik from the drawer, she draped the scarf around the child's blond head and tied another around her waist. She bedecked herself in similar fashion. Then, fluttering their arms, they danced out onto the porch.

Halfway up the steps and holding on to the

iron railing, IdaLee paused. "What have we here?"

Emma Cate giggled into her hands. "We're butterflies, Miss IdaLee. Aren't we bee-yoo-ti-ful?"

Lila smiled at her great-aunt, a frequent visitor since Granny died. IdaLee missed her sister. And Lila didn't mind her company.

The old woman's eyes softened. "Truly beautiful. Both of you girls."

With a quick rat-a-tat-tat, a cascade of water spritzed the side of the house. The three of them jolted. Standing at the front corners, Sam and Deon hosed down the house.

IdaLee ventured deeper into the protective shelter of the porch. "Looks like I got here just in time." She sank onto the porch swing. "Before you became an island and I was cut off."

Rivulets of water flowed off the eaves of the house. Like being in a gazebo during a rainstorm. Or under a waterfall.

Setting the scarves aflutter, Emma Cate twirled around and around. "It's raining, Miss Penry."

"Raining men." Her aunt's wrinkled lips quirked. "Hal-le-lu-jah."

IdaLee cackled at the expression on her face. "Close your mouth, Lila Pat, before you catch flies." Her aunt raised a brow. "Sam Gibson is a fine-looking fellow, don't you think? I may be eighty, but I ain't dead yet."

Never in her entire life had she heard her aunt use anything but correct grammar. She texted in the Queen's English, too.

"Yes, ma'am," she murmured, at a loss to do anything but agree.

"April showers bring May flowers." IdaLee tapped her forefinger on the tip of the little girl's nose. "What do May flowers bring?"

The child perked. "Pilgrims!"

Lila rolled her eyes. "You've been telling that joke at Thanksgiving since I was in preschool."

"Since your father was in preschool, too." IdaLee smirked.

The water stopped streaming off the roof. Drips pitter-pattered onto the steps. Carrying the ladders, Deon, Neil and Rigo headed toward the white van.

The old woman pushed out of the swing. "A good joke is a joke worth retelling."

Lila grabbed her arm to steady her.

Sam slogged over to the bottom of the porch steps. "I've sent the guys home. I'll make sure to leave your yard tidy, though, before I take off."

"Let Emma Cate walk me next door." IdaLee reached for the porch railing. "I made too much applesauce this year. You'd be doing me a favor if you, Lila and your mom took some jars home."

Not giving him a chance to object, she held out her hand to the child.

And that was the way to handle Sam Gibson's delicate pride. *Live and learn, Lila Pat. Live and learn.*

He moved forward to ensure IdaLee made it safely to the ground. "The steps may be slick. I don't want you falling."

Lila's great-aunt threaded her arm through the crook of his elbow. "I don't want to be falling, either."

"I'll be right back," he called over his shoulder.

Ambling inside the house, she found Emma Cate's sketchpad on the island in the kitchen. She put it aside to give to the little girl when she went home. Somewhere, her phone rang.

Searching for her cell, she wandered into the dining room. She was terrible about mislaying her phone. Missing important calls. Suppose it was the panel calling to offer her the residency?

Lila followed the ringing, and then the sound of her own voice into the living room. There was a long beep from the armchair. She pounced.

The decision about the artist-in-residence position wasn't supposed to be until December, but no harm in hoping. Rummaging underneath the cushion, she emerged with her cell in hand. Someone had left a message. It wasn't a California number.

But recognizing the caller, her stomach nose-dived. It was Paige. Taking a deep breath, she hit Play.

"I can't wait to see you, dear Lila. Can you believe my wedding is only three weeks from now?"

Like she needed reminding. She sank into the armchair. Paige rambled on about her prenuptial bliss and bridal cheer.

"…it's going to be the most absolutely glorious wedding ever…"

She closed her eyes.

"…by the way, the calligrapher needs the name of your plus-one by Mon—"

She screamed and dropped the cell. The phone skittered across the hardwood floor.

Moaning, she buried her face in her hands. "No, no, no."

"Lila!" Sam burst into the house. "What's happened?"

She lifted her head.

Chest heaving, his eyes traveled from her face to her phone lying on the floor. "What's wrong?"

Nothing, except she was about to lose what little remained of her self-esteem.

Sam held a Mason jar of pinkish applesauce in his callused palms. "Bad news?"

He had nice hands. Strong, dependable. Hard-working, manly hands.

She reddened. She didn't need to be thinking about his hands. And she really, really didn't want to talk about the situation she'd gotten herself into.

Not with him of all people.

Uncurling from the chair, she extended her hand. "My portion of Aunt IdaLee's applesauce bounty, I presume?"

He handed her the jar. "I stashed the rest in my truck. It was too heavy for Emma Cate to tote, but Miss IdaLee told me to take my time. Said she had something she wanted to show my niece."

"Which reminds me, there's something I wanted to show you."

She trailed into the kitchen. He followed on her heels. Depositing the jar on the counter, she handed him the sketchpad. "Take a look."

"Your illustrations are great." He scrolled through the pages. "Is it for a story?"

"I didn't draw the pictures." She leaned against the island. "Emma Cate drew those this afternoon."

He looked up. "You think they're good?"

"Your niece is four years old." She threw out her hands. "They're remarkable."

He didn't say anything.

"We were creating a story together, and she drew those pictures out of her head." Taking the book from him, Lila turned the pages until she found the right one. "The detail. The intricacy. It's like *Lord of the Rings* meets Narnia."

"I don't know what that means."

"They're exquisitely illustrated, award-winning fantasy tales."

He looked away. "So you're saying she's got talent."

"She has an intuitive sense of space, shape and form. There's no limit to what she could achieve with formal instruction."

He rubbed the back of his neck. "I don't have money for fancy art lessons."

"I wouldn't charge you for—"

"Absolutely not." He reared.

Lila pushed the pad at him. "She has a gift. A God-given gift. He calls people like Emma Cate to capture the beautiful things He has made. And to leave the world a better place."

His mouth went mulish. "Gibsons don't take—"

"—something for nothing," she growled. "So you've said."

But then the most outrageous idea floated across her brain. "Unless you were willing to work out a trade in services."

His eyes narrowed. "The guys are depending on the money from this paint job. I can't—"

"I'm not talking about painting my house."

He cocked his head. "What then?"

"Art lessons for Emma Cate in exchange for something else."

He crossed his arms over his chest. "I don't have anything else to offer."

"Just yourself. And yourself is exactly what I need to solve my Christmas dilemma."

As soon as the words left her mouth, she realized how deranged she must sound. How pathetic. Heat flashed from the top of her head to the soles of her feet.

"You're right." She retreated a step. "It's preposterous. Absurd." She put the island between them. "Forget I said anything. I don't know what possessed me to—"

"What is it you want me to do?"

"Be my plus-one at Paige Lindstrom's December weekend wedding." Inhaling, she pinched her lips together.

"Okay." He dropped his arms. "Deal."

"I don't think you fully understand what I—"

"Date. Paige's wedding. Got it."

She shook her head so hard, her curls bounced. "Not a date. My plus-one. My escort for the weekend."

"Call it what you will." He stuck his tongue in his cheek. "But I don't think 'escort' is the message you want to convey, do you, Lila Pat?"

"This isn't funny, Samuel Gibson."

His mouth curved. "No, I can see that it's not."

"Besides, it's not practical." She grimaced. "Did I forget to mention I'm the maid of honor?"

He leaned his elbows on the island. "Why don't you think it's doable?"

"It involves going out of town Friday through Sunday for wedding party activities." She gave him a helpless, hopeless shrug. "You have Emma Cate to care for."

Eyes stinging, her gaze darted from the refrigerator to the microwave, looking for a place to land. Anywhere to avoid the pity she was certain she'd find on his face.

"Which weekend in December?"

Her gaze flitted back to him. "W-what?"

"The first weekend in December? Some people from our class mentioned they were going."

She nodded. "It's the first weekend."

He slapped his hand on the counter. She jumped.

"That's perfect then."

"Why is that perfect?"

"That weekend Emma Cate goes to stay with her other grandparents for a week. They'll celebrate their own Christmas."

His grin set butterflies, prancing ponies and dolphins to dancing in her belly.

"I'd love to be your plus-one at Paige's wedding."

What had she done? Her heart spasmed. Sam glorious Gibson—her plus-one. Was she out of her mind?

And once he fully understood the ramifications of what he'd committed himself to, he'd back out. Leaving her high and dry. She felt sick to her stomach.

This was a disaster in the making. This wasn't going to end well for her. This wasn't going to end well at all.

Chapter Four

"Lila!" After the church service on Sunday morning, Sam hurried out of the pew and into the aisle. "Wait up."

But he wasn't quick enough. She'd already slipped outside. He rushed after her.

"Hey!" On the steps, he caught hold of her sleeve, stopping her headlong flight. "Where's the fire?"

Shoulders slumping, she turned to face him. "Oh. Hi." Her remarkable gray-blue eyes darted as the congregation spilled out of the sanctuary.

He got the distinct impression she'd been trying to avoid him. Why, he couldn't imagine. Unless—his lungs constricted—she was ashamed to be seen with him.

Sure, he was working for her, but in high school she'd never been one of those two-faced, shallow, mean girls. She'd been kind to everyone.

Or maybe her sudden reluctance went deeper than that. Would he never live down the shame of what his father had done?

Sam squared his shoulders. "We need to talk."

Her gaze returned and found his. "Okay. Go ahead." As if bracing for a blow, she raised her chin.

A breeze lifted a strand of her hair. He had the sudden impulse to brush the springy, silken curl from her face. To coil the ringlet around his index finger.

Then, horrified he might have actually said that out loud, he rubbed his hand over his mouth. "I need to know what color you want to paint your house."

"Paint?" She blinked at him. "That's what you wanted to talk to me about?" Her voice went high at the end.

"Yeah." He cocked his head. "What did you think I was going to say?"

"Nothing." She smiled. "Sure. Paint."

The knot loosened in his belly. And he told himself to stop being so ridiculously insecure. If Lila Penry was ashamed to be seen with him, she wouldn't have asked him to be her plus-one at Paige's wedding. He needed to get out of his own head. And focus on the job for which he was being paid.

"I'll need to buy paint midweek."

She frowned. "I haven't given the color much thought."

He arched his brow. "And you call yourself an artist?"

She smacked his arm.

He grinned. "I'm not the artsy kind of painter, but I'll be happy to share what I know about exterior colors."

She released a breath. "That would be great."

"How about we meet Monday afternoon at the paint store? You can tell me what you're envisioning, and we can go from there."

"Good." She took a step away. "See you then."

He headed toward the educational wing to collect Emma Cate from children's church. Dwight Fleming, owner of a rafting company, called out a greeting. Fleming was Cliff Penry's brother-in-law, and Sam had painted Fleming's house last spring. Jake McAbee stopped to thank him for the great job the crew had done at the Apple Valley Orchard.

Church people weren't at all what he'd supposed growing up. He hadn't known much about God until the past few years. No surprise, his father hadn't been a churchgoer. And his mom had often been too overwhelmed by illness to bring him or his sister.

But as soon as Emma Cate came into his life, he realized he needed not only divine assistance to be the sort of father she deserved, but he also needed the support of the people at Truelove Community. Everyone at church had been welcoming. So now he and his niece were learning about faith together.

Later that afternoon, Sam and Emma Cate hiked to a nearby waterfall. One of his favorite spots in the Pisgah National Forest. Not far from Truelove. Just off the beaten path.

The mornings and evenings had grown chilly, but the afternoons were warm. Perfect conditions for fall foliage. And painting Lila's house.

Settling down, he leaned against the hard granite of a giant boulder and watched his niece play along the edge of the glen. The forest floor was strewn with the fallen leaves and bracken of previous winters. The sound of the waterfall roared in his ears.

He liked to imagine the spot his own private Eden. Undiscovered by the rest of the world. As a boy, he'd stumbled upon the place by accident.

An oasis of calm and peace. In times of distress or joy, it had become his personal refuge. He'd never brought anyone here but Emma Cate. She loved being outdoors.

Indian summer had pushed peak leaf color into November this year. The usual hordes of leaf peepers from all over the world had come and gone from the nearby Blue Ridge Parkway.

Mountain folk had the autumn splendor to themselves once more. And even this late—the last full week before Thanksgiving—the foliage was a sight to behold.

Once the expected storm front arrived, the trees would probably drop their leaves all at once.

But today the mountains were still ablaze with color. A visual feast. He wasn't a romantic or contemplative sort of guy. But there was something achingly beautiful about these mountains. Especially this time of year. Each season brought a different, yet altogether wonderful, kind of beauty to his favorite place.

Inexplicably, his thoughts flew to a certain landscape artist. And he imagined her standing in the glen after the first snowfall of winter. The evergreens bedaubed with snow. The flash of a cardinal against heavy-laden branches. Icicles dripping. And other than the muted trickle of the falls, a hushed stillness.

Clutching a handful of leaves, Emma Cate flopped down beside him. "Which one is your favorite, Daddy Sam?" Like a merchant displaying her wares, she fanned out her collection on the blue plaid blanket for his inspection.

She held up a vivid yellow.

He smiled. "That one would be Mawmaw's favorite."

She twirled an almost otherworldly shade of

orange between her fingers. "I like this one the best."

Lifting the crimson-red leaf, he was again reminded of Lila Penry. And the glorious shade of her hair.

"Which one, Daddy Sam?"

"I—I… I guess this one is my favorite." He gulped.

"Christmas will be here soon." She sighed with happiness. "I love Christmas, Daddy Sam."

His childhood—and Christmas—had more often than not been bleak. He never used to care much for the holidays. But thanks to steady work this year, he'd finally be able to purchase the dollhouse he hadn't been able to give Emma Cate on her birthday.

She never asked for anything, but he'd seen how her gaze fastened on it during visits to the big box store on the highway. Yet she seemed to sense money was tight. She might not have everything so many children in Truelove took for granted, but she appeared content as long as she had him.

Eyes shining, she smiled at him. "I love you, Daddy Sam."

Unaccustomed moisture stung his eyelids. "I love you, too."

Planting a quick kiss on top of her head, he got

to his feet. "We better start heading back, baby doll. Before the light goes."

Time to get home and prepare for another workweek.

Late Monday afternoon, he pulled in to the Sherwin-Williams lot and found Lila's green Mini Cooper already there. He bit back a smile. The quirky vehicle was so her.

She'd been at school all day. He'd spent the morning making repairs on her house and replacing rotten fascia boards.

Inside the store, he found her examining paint chips. "What are you thinking?"

"I don't know what I'm thinking. That's the problem."

"We can always paint it white again."

She shook her head, and her loose red curls quivered. "I want color. I just don't know which color."

"Close your eyes."

Eyes widening, she did the exact opposite. "What? Why?"

"Trust me." He took hold of her shoulders. Her black cashmere sweater was soft beneath his palms. "Close your eyes. Imagine you're standing outside your grandmother's house."

A tiny vein pulsed in the hollow of her throat, but she closed her eyes. "Okay," she rasped. "Now what?"

Funny, he'd never noticed the fullness in her bottom lip. And her upper lip had a pleasing bow shape.

"Sam?"

A delicious fruity fragrance wafted off her hair.

"Sorry." He swallowed. "I want you to visualize your favorite memory of your grandmother's house."

Lila lifted her cheeks.

"Keep your eyes closed." He waited a few seconds. "What do you see?"

"I see sunny yellow daffodils in the border along the picket fence." Her forehead creased. Her eyelids remained shut. "I see lavender-blue hydrangea snowballs against the stone foundation. Also, white rhododendrons with waxy green leaves. And Granny's crimson-red roses."

His mouth went dry. He'd gotten home Sunday afternoon to discover the red leaf from the glen tucked into his jacket pocket. When had he done that? And why? Accidentally or on purpose?

Lila's eyes popped open. "Soft white for the trim and a buttery yellow for the body of the house." She smiled. "Wow. That was quite the mind trick." Her lashes fluttered.

His heart slammed against his breastbone.

All at once, he realized how close they were standing to each other.

He dropped his hands. "Let's look at the yellow chips." He moved toward the display.

"There's so many of them," she groaned.

"Paint tends to dry slightly darker than the color on the card. So how about this one?" He pulled a chip from the stack. "Or that one?" He held the two colors side by side for her to compare.

"I don't know which to choose. It shouldn't be this hard for an art person like me to decide."

She shook her head. Her hair danced again. As did something inside his rib cage.

"It's a big decision. But you like these two the best?"

She nodded.

"I have an idea." He straightened. "Would an art person like yourself happen to have any foam board lying around the house?"

Her lovely mouth quirked. "This art person might just have a piece or two of foam board lying around the house."

Going to the counter, he gave the clerk the paint numbers. They waited for the machine to mix the right color combinations. And he bought a quart-size sample of each.

Back at the house, while she rummaged through her studio, he went around the perimeter to check on the crew's progress.

Deon was packing up. "Should finish the

caulking tomorrow. Neil will be done with taping then, too."

Rigo hauled a folded ladder to the van. "We'll
be ready to paint Wednesday morning."

Now, if only he could get Lila to make up her
mind about the color. Hearing her call, he left
the guys.

On the front steps, she handed him the white
foam-core board. "Don't you have to get Emma
Cate from after-school care soon?"

"I've got a few minutes before I'm due there."

She hoisted the strap of her portfolio case on
her shoulder. "I have a watercolor class to teach
at the rec center this evening."

"I'm going to paint half the board with each
of the yellows. They should be dry by the time
you get home tonight. I'll leave them by the door
for you to compare."

She bit the inside of her cheek. "When do you
need my decision?"

He broadened his chest. "Yesterday."

She rolled her eyes.

"Text me which color you prefer. Number one
or number two. I plan to buy the paint first thing
Wednesday morning as soon as the store opens.
Got that?"

She saluted him. "Aye, aye, Captain."

The shimmery silken scarf she'd draped

around her shoulders brought out the flecks of silver—and the mischief—in her eyes.

His pulse jump-started. "See you tomorrow, Penry."

Fluttering her fingers, she came down the steps, passing him. "Not if I see you first, Gibson." She laughed to let him know she was kidding and headed for her car in the driveway.

Not moving from where she left him on the porch, he watched her reverse to the street and drive away. What concerned him more than anything was how much he found himself looking forward to seeing her tomorrow.

The swirl of anticipation, an unfamiliar emotion, left him feeling more than a little unsettled. Leaning against the railing, he broke into a cold sweat. He hadn't stopped to think before he agreed to be her plus-one. So why had he?

Because of the art lessons for Emma Cate, of course. He'd do anything to make sure she had the advantages he'd never had. And taking Lila to the wedding wasn't exactly a hardship.

In high school, she'd been quiet whenever he was near. Reserved. Often tongue-tied. A little uptight, which now he realized hid a sweet shyness.

Until last weekend, he'd had no idea how amusing Lila Penry was. She made him laugh. She was fun to be around.

As his mother was fond of telling him, he could use more fun in his life. Which was great. As long as both of them kept it light and casual. After the wedding, they'd go their separate ways. Back to their normal routine.

Which was fine by him. His smile faltered. Wasn't it?

He'd dated a few women while in the Navy. Nothing serious. Never interested in anyone beyond a second date. After the disaster of his parents' marriage, he doubted he'd make good husband material anyway. Then Emma Cate came into his life.

And he felt an additional weight of responsibility for ensuring the guys had the means to support their families. His life was already complicated enough without adding a relationship into the mix. Although, in truth, life had always been complicated for him.

He pinched the bridge of his nose. It wouldn't do to get emotionally involved with Emma Cate's art teacher. It wouldn't do at all.

Good plan. He exhaled. Glad he'd had the foresight to work through all that in his head before they went to the wedding.

No harm. No foul. No surprises. No problem.

The next days passed in a blur of activity. Lila decided on a color. On Wednesday, the crew spray-painted the body of the house.

It ended up being a long workday. She insisted on upholding her end of their wedding bargain by picking up Emma Cate after school and bringing her to the house for an art lesson.

She also insisted on feeding his niece dinner. He'd let the other guys go to make it home in time for supper with their own families. The hours of light were already shortened.

After packing the last of his tools in the truck, he knocked on the door.

Emma Cate let him into the house. "Look what Miss Penry showed me how to draw today, Daddy Sam!"

Holding up a pen-and-ink sketch for him to admire, she gyrated around him. Braids dancing. A whirlwind of energy. And fluttery color.

Emma Cate had been into Lila's scarf collection again.

"She has a whimsical style all her own." Lila came out of the kitchen, a wrapped paper plate in her hands. "I saved you some dinner."

He scowled. "You didn't have to do that."

"I know, but I did." She thrust the plate at him and glared. "Deal with it."

"Thank you." Stomach rumbling, he decided there was no point in refusing her generosity. He'd only hurt her feelings. And there was no sense in letting good food go to waste. "Get your jacket, Emma Cate."

Lila helped the little girl slip her arms into the puffy pink coat.

"Tomorrow we'll paint the trim. Two coats. On Friday, we'll reattach the gutters. Then we'll be ready to scrape and clean the windows. And none too soon. The storm front is supposed to roll in Saturday night."

She straightened Emma Cate's collar. "Don't forget your book bag, sweetie."

The child scurried toward the dining room.

He reached behind him for the door handle. "One more thing. Did you want me to put a new coat of paint on the front door? Same as the trim?"

Lila's eyes went deer-in-the-headlights. "I—I don't know. I haven't thought about it." She cocked her head. "Did Callie McAbee keep her front door the same apple red?"

"She did."

"Good. I can't imagine Apple Valley Orchard without that welcoming red door." Lila sighed. "Doors are important. Doors say something about the personality of the home." She looked at him. "What should I do?"

"Are you happy with the yellow base coat on the house?"

"Very happy. It's beautiful. Exactly as I envisioned."

Good to hear. Word of mouth from a happy client meant another future client in the making.

"Would you trust me to pick the door color?" Leaning against the wall, he crossed his arms. "I have a sense of what you like and don't like. I think I could find something to reflect your personality and fit the vibe of the house."

"Houses have vibes?"

The house he'd grown up in had, and its vibe hadn't been good.

His gaze darted to the fireplace in the living room. To the tasteful splashes of color from the pillows on the couch. To the throw casually draped over the back. And to the warmth of the kitchen beyond. "Definitely."

The vibe of this house shouted *home*. Everything he wished he'd had as a boy. Everything he was determined that one day Emma Cate would enjoy.

He jutted his jaw. "Do you trust me to make the choice or not?"

An easy curve to her lips, her eyes lifted to meet his. "I trust you."

Something tore inside his chest.

The drawing tucked under her arm, his niece rejoined them. Jerking them both out of the vibe that suddenly pulsed between them. He cleared his throat.

"I'll paint the door Saturday morning, then."

He drew Emma Cate up against him. "But you can't see it until it's dry. We'll have the final reveal that afternoon."

"Dad's the executor of Granny's estate. I'll tell him to stop by with your check."

Over the next couple of days, he put a great deal of consideration into what color to select for the front door. He arrived Saturday morning, reminding Lila of her promise not to peek, and confined her to the back of the house. Leaving the door ajar, he positioned a drop cloth underneath to protect the hardwood floor in the foyer.

Sam dipped the bristles of the brush into the high-gloss paint.

With the cool wind whipping off the mountain, it wouldn't take long for the paint to dry. In the meantime, he busied himself fixing a loose board he'd noticed on Lila's back deck.

"Can I look yet?" she called from the kitchen.

He wandered inside. "Impatient much, Penry? You'd think it was Christmas morning." He moved around the island. "You stay here." He wagged his finger. "I'll check and then come get you."

"Fine," she muttered.

Sam was on the porch when Cliff Penry's sedan pulled up next to the curb. Closing the door behind him, he loped into the kitchen again. "The paint's dry, and your dad is here."

Her eyes lit. "Let's go."

"Wait."

She gave him a pouty, sideways look. And his insides did a nosedive. What was with him?

But he figured she probably didn't realize how cute she looked. Or the fallout it had on his equilibrium.

"I want you to get the full effect, so let's go out the back and around the house to see it."

"Whatever." She grabbed hold of his sleeve. "Move it already."

She lugged him around the corner of the house. He had a split second of uncertainty. Suppose she didn't like it?

As long as he got paid, he didn't usually care what color his customers chose. Yet somehow this job felt different. Maybe because of their friendship? Or based on their limited previous acquaintance, perhaps because he and Lila had finally *become* friends.

True to her word, she kept her gaze turned away from the house as they approached her father. "Hi, Dad."

"Mr. Penry, sir."

They joined him at the top of the stone steps leading to the street. The best perspective from which to view the house. He'd invested more of himself in this project than in any other he'd ever done. But no matter why he cared, what she thought was important.

His Adam's apple bobbed in his throat. "You can turn around now, Lila."

Rotating as gracefully as a door opening on its hinges, she gasped. "Oh."

His stomach bottomed out. She didn't like it. "I—I can repaint it another color."

"Repaint it? No..." Her hands flew to her mouth. "I love it. The color is just right. A soft apple green." Her luminous eyes locked onto his. "You got me. It's perfect."

Sam got a little lost in her gaze until he remembered Cliff Penry—her father—was also standing there. "Uh, what do you think, Mr. Penry?"

Her dad's eyes cut between them before resting on the house. "You washed the windows and touched up the lanterns, too?"

"Yes, sir."

Folding his arms across his sweater-vest, Penry rocked on his heels. "I think it looks amazing. Well done, Gibson. I see why you have such a great reputation."

His heart hammered. Fifteen years after his father swindled half the town out of their life savings, earning Mr. Penry's respect—and Truelove's—meant the world to him. Better than money in the bank.

But Cliff Penry wasn't finished surprising him.

"Myra and I would love to have you and your family join us for Thanksgiving dinner next week at Aunt IdaLee's." Lila's father cradled his chin in his hand. "Unless your mother has already made plans."

His eyes flicked to Lila. It appeared to be the first time she was hearing the invite, too. Yet she didn't look displeased.

"Actually, Mom and my stepfather, Phil, are spending Thanksgiving with his folks in Tennessee. It's their first Thanksgiving together."

Mr. Penry stuck his hands in his trouser pockets. "Have you made other plans with Emma Cate?"

"No, sir." He'd heard that a cafeteria, about an hour away in Asheville, served Thanksgiving dinner. "Not really."

"That settles it, then." Penry clapped him across his shoulder blades. "We'd be honored to have you join us, son. Plan on arriving about eleven. We eat at noon."

Again, his gaze sought Lila's. A tiny smile hovered at the corners of her lips. She gave him a slight nod.

He angled to her father. "The honor is mine. What can I bring?"

"Not a thing." Penry dug the check from his pocket. "Just bring yourself."

Frowning, he widened his stance. "I don't—"

"We need dinner rolls." She threw him a wry look. "Can you bring dinner rolls, Sam?"

He allowed himself a small smile. "Dinner rolls I can bring."

She smirked. "Fantastic."

He might've painted the door her dream color, but apparently the connection—friendship?—went both ways. A new and surprising thought. She got him, too.

And suddenly, he wasn't sure whether that was a good thing. Or if, instead, he ought to be terrified.

Chapter Five

Overnight, a cold wind began to blow. The temperature plummeted. And just like that, winter fell upon Truelove.

With only a few days in the school week, as usual the children were restless. Already anticipating the break.

Early on Thanksgiving morning, Lila went next door to help her great-aunt get the house ready for the guests. She carefully positioned the turkey on the oven rack to cook.

Her cousins and her parents would bring different family favorites. A few hours later, her mom and dad arrived with several casseroles.

From a chair at the table, Aunt IdaLee sat like a queen on her throne, supervising the menu. Around 10:00 a.m., AnnaBeth, her husband, Jonas, and their little boy, Hunter, arrived. In the flurry of removing coats, AnnaBeth drew Lila over to the side.

"You and I need to talk about that mysterious text message you sent me this week." AnnaBeth made air quotes with her fingers. "'Plus-one mission accomplished.'" She folded her arms across her sweater. "So spill."

Eyes darting to make sure no one in her nosy family overheard them, she pulled AnnaBeth into IdaLee's front parlor. "This has to stay between you and me."

She poked her head out into the hallway to make sure no one was listening, but everyone had drifted into the kitchen, enticed by delicious aromas of turkey and stuffing.

"Don't leave me hanging." AnnaBeth reeled her back into the room. "Who's your plus-one?"

Lila pursed her lips. "This information is strictly need-to-know."

"Why?" She frowned. "Is it someone terrible?"

"No." Lila made a face. "The opposite, actually."

"Ooh. I'm intrigued." AnnaBeth's lips twitched. "Why the secrecy, then?"

"Because…" She gulped. "He's the exact opposite of terrible, and I don't want my family to embarrass him."

"Why would they embarrass him?"

"He's so out of my league, A.B." Lila bit her lip. "I don't want my parents making a big deal out of us going to the wedding together. He's doing me a huge favor by going as my plus-one."

"Out of your league?" AnnaBeth sniffed. "I doubt that. Maybe it's the other way around. Getting to be seen with you is a huge favor to him."

She gave AnnaBeth a reluctant smile. "This is why I love you, but trust me. Going to Paige's wedding with klutzy, frizzy-haired me is on no one's bucket list, much less his."

AnnaBeth scowled. "I don't like when you talk that way. I wish you would see yourself like everyone else sees you. A loyal friend. Kind." She ticked off the list on her fingers. "Smart. Funny. Talented. The girl with such lovely hair."

"You're sweet. Thank you. You almost had me…" She rolled her eyes. "Until the hair part."

AnnaBeth touched her arm. "Don't make the mistake I did in letting your insecurities define you. God says we are fearfully and wonderfully made."

It never ceased to amaze Lila that her confident, wonderful friend had once struggled with body image issues. Until Jonas's love and God's peace gave her a new perspective.

Her heart understood AnnaBeth was speaking truth, but somehow the truth didn't make it to her head. Instead, all too often what she heard was the voice of the mean girl in the second grade who first made fun of her hair.

Lila shrugged. "Promise you'll keep this development to yourself."

Her friend laid her hand over the region of her heart. "Debutante's honor." A smile tugged at her lips.

The deb thing had been a funny romantic joke between AnnaBeth and Jonas when she first arrived in Truelove.

"I don't want anyone making false assumptions about the true nature of our relationship."

"The true nature—Oh." AnnaBeth nodded. "You mean the matchmakers. But you're going to tell your parents, right?"

"Eventually..." Lila looked at her sideways. "Maybe when we arrive at the resort."

"Okay. Enough disclaimers. I'm dying of curiosity." AnnaBeth rubbed her palms together. "Who is your plus-one?"

"It's Sam." She hung her head. "Sam Gibson."

Grabbing both of Lila's arms, AnnaBeth did an excited little staccato with her high-heeled boots on the hardwood floor. "My heart forever belongs to a certain rancher. But Sam? Sam Gibson's so... So..."

Lila's gaze shot up. "Yummy." She grimaced. "Yeah, I know." She wrung her hands. "What have I done, AnnaBeth? What have I done?"

"Nonsense." AnnaBeth raised her chin. "It's going to be great. What can I do to help?"

"Paige is in charge of getting our dresses from the final fitting to the wedding." Lila slumped. "But then there's the rest of the weekend. I have nothing Sam-worthy to wear and no money to outfit my wedding weekend wardrobe."

"On it." AnnaBeth waved her hand. "Not a problem."

"Where have you girls gotten to?" Lila's mother called. "We could use help with the pies."

Taking hold of Lila's elbow, AnnaBeth steered her toward the kitchen. "My mom and dad are coming to the ranch tonight to spend the rest of the holiday weekend with us. My mom and I were planning to go shopping in Asheville. You should come with us."

She stared at her friend. "Black Friday shopping with your mom?"

"Trust me when I tell you my mom will have your wardrobe sorted in no time. For pennies on the dollar." AnnaBeth smirked. "If there was a spiritual gift for shopping, my mom would have it."

AnnaBeth's mother, Victoria, was indeed a fashionista.

Outside the kitchen, Lila nudged her friend. "The apple doesn't fall far from the tree."

"We do what we can to make the world a better place."

Lila grinned. "One fashion makeover at a time."

"Have you heard from California?"

She shook her head. "A few weeks to go yet before there's any word."

AnnaBeth chewed at her lower lip. "Be careful, friend."

"What do you mean?"

"First, the residency program and now your plus-one." AnnaBeth squeezed her arm. "Secrets have a way of blowing up in your face. And at the worst possible time. I don't want you to get hurt."

Before Lila could respond, they were pulled into the organized chaos of Thanksgiving dinner preparations, and there was no further time to chat.

She kept her eye on the kitchen clock, anxiously awaiting Sam and Emma Cate's arrival. But when the doorbell chimed, she nearly jumped out of her skin.

"Best set the turkey pan on the counter before you drop it, Lila Pat." Aunt IdaLee raised her eyebrow. "And go greet Samuel."

She didn't dare risk a look at AnnaBeth. But Lila caught the glance exchanged between her mother and her great-aunt. Cheeks flaming, she shed the oven mitts and hurried toward the front of the house.

Lila walked in on her dad introducing Sam to her cousin, Jonas, and Hunter. He already knew most of her family. Truelove was a small town. Way too small.

Emma Cate, her eyes the same brilliant blue as Sam's, hung back, pressed against his side.

"Hey, Emma Cate." Cute little cowboy Hunter twirled his hat around and around on his index finger. "Want to come see me lasso Aunt Ida-Lee's lions?"

The stone lions guarded either side of the porch steps. A rope hung from his belt. A pint-size roping champion, Hunter carried the lasso with him everywhere.

Emma Cate unglued herself from Sam. "Okay." She smiled at Hunter.

The children turned toward the door. Sam frowned. Jonas reached for the brass knob. "Hunter knows to stay on the porch, but I'll supervise until dinner's ready just to be sure."

"Dinner rolls, I presume?" Lila took the cellophane bag from Sam.

"You presume correctly." His mouth quirked, but his eyes followed Emma Cate and five-year-old Hunter out the door. "Did I just lose my girl to a cowboy?"

Lila laughed. "Everybody loves a cowboy."

Blue eyes gleaming in amusement, he hitched his brow. "Is that so?"

She blushed.

Actually, she preferred quarterbacks turned sailors turned paint contractors. But she'd give up chocolate, coffee and her entire collection of hair products before ever admitting to that.

It was her dad who inadvertently came to her rescue.

"On Thanksgiving Day, we generally help Aunt IdaLee decorate for Christmas." He placed his hand on Sam's shoulder. "I wondered if you'd help me get her box of ornaments out of the attic?"

Sam nodded. "I'd be glad to, sir. Lead the way."

It wasn't long after they went upstairs that Jonas brought Emma Cate to the kitchen. She'd grown bored throwing the rope.

"I not good like Hunter."

Lila hugged her. "Not even Hunter's dad is as good as Hunter."

"Hey," Jonas gave her mock frown. "I resent that remark."

"Although you have many admirable qualities, roping isn't one of them. You, my love," Anna-Beth gave him a quick peck on his cheek, "totally resemble that remark."

He laughed. "Such abuse. I'm going to rejoin my son." He reached for one of the butterscotch brownies on a plate. "But before I go—"

"Don't ruin your dinner." IdaLee lightly smacked his hand. "We'll let you know when it's time to eat."

Flapping her apron, the old woman shooed him out of the kitchen.

Lila took Emma Cate's hand. "I think I know one thing you would be fabulous at. Let's set the table together."

Aunt IdaLee shuffled to the dining room ahead of them. "I'll pull the silver from the sideboard."

Lila showed the little girl how to fold and place the Thanksgiving-themed paper napkins on the left side on the plate.

A tiny line creased Emma Cate's brow. "Where's Daddy Sam?"

"He's upstairs helping my dad bring down some boxes."

The child seemed to accept her explanation, but Lila noticed she continued to shoot side-long glances toward the stairs. Concentrating on aligning the edges of the napkin, Emma Cate caught her bottom lip in her teeth.

At the sound of feet clomping down the stairs, she abandoned the napkins and peered into the foyer. "It's Daddy Sam," she called over her shoulder to Lila. "Hey, Daddy Sam. I'm helping Miss Penry fold de turkey napkins."

Toting a large cardboard box, he paused in the

doorway. "So I see." He glanced at Lila. "She's being a good helper, I hope?"

Lila smiled. "The best."

"Good to hear." He shifted the box in his arms. "Let me finish helping Miss Penry's dad, baby doll. I'll be back soon."

"Okay, Daddy Sam." She skipped over to Lila at the long mahogany table and folded another napkin. "He likes me to call him Daddy Sam."

Lila went behind the child, placing a fork on top of each napkin. IdaLee followed with the butter knife and spoon.

Emma Cate moved on to the next place setting. "But in my head, I call him Daddy and at school, too. Like de udder girls."

Midmotion, Lila froze. Her gaze flicked to her great-aunt. The old woman's mouth pursed.

"Attachment issues," her aunt whispered. "And I'm not talking about the child. Nothing that love can't cure, though."

IdaLee raised her voice. "Emma Cate, would you walk into the kitchen and tell the ladies I think we're ready to call everyone to the table?"

"Yes, ma'am." Giving them a bright smile, the little girl scurried away.

Unbidden tears misted Lila's eyes. "She's such a sweetheart."

"Reminds me of Samuel when he was her age." Her aunt gave her a sad smile. "Never the same after what his father did, but he's made the most and more of what the good Lord gave him."

Taking a breath, IdaLee patted her arm. "But never you fear, the matchmakers have got someone special picked out for him."

Hang on. Someone special? For Sam… Swaying slightly, she blinked to clear her vision.

"Are you feeling all right, Lila Pat?" IdaLee glanced at the fork she still clutched in her hand. "Goodness, child. Not so tight. Don't want to leave a mark on your skin." Her aunt bustled toward the kitchen.

Only then did Lila realize the prongs were digging into her flesh. She relaxed her grip. She should warn him he was on borrowed time. That he was a marked man.

Firmly setting the last fork in its place, she decided she'd have to make sure she and Sam got the chance to talk later.

And was that the only reason she wanted a private word with him? The infernal, annoying voice of the girl from the second grade brayed in her ear. *Think again.*

Of course, that's why she wanted to talk to him. Warning him was the kind thing to do. The friend thing to do.

Everyone trooped into the dining room to claim their seats. Per tradition, IdaLee sat at one end of the table, and Lila's father at the other.

"Would it be all right if Emma Cate sat between me and Hunter?" Lila's mother beamed at Sam. "It's been far too long since I've had the pleasure of a little girl's company."

Somehow it worked out that Lila found herself seated next to her father with Sam across the table from her.

His eyes scanned the length of the table, practically groaning with food. At the sound of Emma Cate's silvery laughter, for a second there was this look on Sam's face... A look she wasn't sure how to interpret. At the beginning of the meal, he was quiet, but her father and Jonas soon got him talking about the upcoming college football bowls.

After dinner in another IdaLee-decreed tradition, the men retired to the kitchen to handle the cleanup and do the dishes.

In a rush of cold air, Jonas's mom, Deirdre, breezed into the house. "Happy Thanksgiving, everyone. We come bearing Aunt IdaLee's Christmas tree."

This year, Deirdre and her husband, Dwight Fleming, had eaten Thanksgiving dinner with his daughter's family across town.

Sam and Jonas went outside to help Jonas's stepfather wrangle the fir tree out of his truck and into the living room.

Once the tree was secured into the tree stand,

Dwight clapped his brother-in-law, Cliff, across his back. "I'm ready for a slice of Myra's pecan pie now."

"Coming right up." Lila's father moved with him toward the kitchen. "Thanks for stopping by the tree farm and picking up Aunt IdaLee's tree. With all these young folks on the job, I think our work is done."

"Just until you get to your own house, Cliff Penry," her mother chimed in. "Our decorations are going up tomorrow, rain or shine."

Everyone laughed.

Smiling, her dad glanced at his aunt IdaLee. "I'm guessing you have a plan of attack?"

The old lady sniffed. "Did Eisenhower?"

She set Jonas and AnnaBeth to stringing lights. "Emma Cate and Hunter, y'all rummage through the ornament boxes over there." Ida-Lee motioned to the older women. "If you two wouldn't mind wrapping the gifts upstairs in my sewing room. I think you'll find everything labeled."

IdaLee swung around to Sam. "Everyone earns their keep around here, young man."

"Wouldn't have it any other way." He grinned. "Put me to work, Miss IdaLee."

Lila bit back a smile.

If he knew what the old woman and her cronies had in store for him, he'd hightail it out of the house this very instant. She had to hand it to her maiden aunt, though. She knew how to handle Sam Gibson.

"Lila Pat, get your coat." Her aunt waved an imperious hand. "You and Samuel can wrap the garland and twinkle lights across the porch."

She'd been wishing for a chance to talk with him alone. *About the target on his back, thank you very much, second-grade girl.* And as if reading her mind—a frightening notion—Aunt IdaLee had handed Lila the perfect opportunity for a quiet word with Sam.

Out on the porch, she wound the garland around the railing while he tackled the thin gingerbread columns. The tangy scent of the pine boughs filled the brisk air. They worked together for a while in companionable silence. The wind had died down somewhat, but in a steady, whirling dance, leaves drifted downward to cover the ground.

"Thank you for sharing your Thanksgiving with us. Our holidays were never like this. My mother did her best, but..." He bent his head to the task. "This is what I want Emma Cate's childhood memories to be—full of happiness, laughter and family."

Did she dare tell him of her earlier conversation with Emma Cate? This was delicate territory. But she sensed the issue with Emma Cate needed to be addressed. She'd have to tread lightly.

"Can I ask you something, Sam?"

He secured a swoop of garland to the wooden railing. "Sure."

When she didn't answer right away, he looked up. "What?"

She bit her lip. "It's absolutely none of my business, but Emma Cate said something earlier, and it's bothered me ever since."

"Tell me." He straightened. "I want to know."

"Why did you tell Emma Cate to call you Daddy Sam?"

"Because Uncle Sam's already claimed?" He gave her a teasing grin, but his eyes slid away, and she knew he was hedging the truth.

She told him what Emma Cate secretly called him. "Because that's what the other little girls call their fathers."

His mouth went mulish. "Emma Cate has a father, and I'm not him." He turned away.

"Sam."

A grudging look on his face, he angled back.

"Her biological father died two years ago. She doesn't remember him. You're the only father she'll ever know."

"Emma Cate's dad was a great father and husband." Sam stuffed his hands in his pockets. "It kills me she doesn't remember him." His Adam's apple bobbed. "Or my sister, her mother, either."

Lila touched his coat sleeve. "But oh, how wonderful that God put you into her life."

He looked up. "You think so?"

"I also think there might be a deeper reason why you won't let her call you Daddy."

He stiffened. "Like what?"

"Like a commitment issue."

A nerve jumped in his jaw. "You're right. This isn't any of your business." He pushed off from the railing.

"Wait. Please." She stepped in front of him. "Don't be offended. I meant Emma Cate might believe you're not committed to her."

Sam threw out his hands. "I left the Navy to take care of Emma Cate. I never intended to return to Truelove, but I did so she could be close to Mom. Emma Cate knows how much she means to me."

"Yet Emma Cate seems anxious whenever you're out of her sight. Like she's afraid she's going to lose you."

Pain jabbed his heart. "Just like she lost her parents," he rasped.

"I'm sorry." She snagged hold of his hand. "I shouldn't have said anything."

His shoulders slumped. "But you believe it to be true."

"I think qualifying 'Daddy' with 'Sam' makes her feel her time with you isn't permanent. That unlike the other girls, she doesn't belong to anyone." Lila locked eyes with him. "I understand about not fitting in. Feeling like an outsider."

He ground his teeth. "I never wanted her to feel that way. After what my father did... I've felt like an outsider, too."

Sam could tell from her expression he'd surprised her.

"But you were the star quarterback who put Truelove High on the map. Taking us to the state championship."

He looked at her. "Can I tell you something I've never told anyone else?"

Lila put her hand to her throat. "Of course. I'd never betray your trust."

Sam scrubbed his hand over his face. "I didn't like playing football."

"Hold on. I must have misheard. I thought you said—"

"Do you know who gave me my first football and taught me how to throw?" He laughed, but the sound contained no mirth. "My father. Football was something *he* loved. And then when I was eleven, he skipped town."

"Why did you play all through high school, then?"

"Honestly? Because I wanted to prove to him—wherever he was—and to this town that I was better than him. A better player than he'd ever been." His lips twisted. "A better man. A better father. A better everything."

Perhaps prove it to himself, too? A new and uncomfortable thought.

"You already are. And a good man, too."

He shook his head. "That's why I pushed myself as a teenager. I knew I was good enough for college ball, but I turned down the scholarships because Mom had a lot of overdue medical bills."

"So you joined the military."

"The Navy offered a regular salary." He shrugged. "And I needed to get out of town."

Lila broke eye contact. "Did it work?"

"Running away, you mean?" He grimaced. "You can call it what it was. And no, it didn't work."

"You don't know how appealing running away sounds."

"We take our baggage wherever we go. And I never wanted for Emma Cate to carry mine." His chest heaved. "Have I ruined her for good?"

"Not at all." Her gaze probed his features. "You can fix this. Love can fix this. Reassure her of your love. Help her to feel safe in your love."

Emma Cate burst out onto the porch. "Daddy Sam."

He winced.

"Miss Penry. Daddy Sam. Come see Miss Ida-Lee's tree."

In her gentle way, Lila had danced around the real problem. The commitment issue was his. And he needed to make things right.

He exchanged a look with Lila. "You go ahead. Emma Cate and I will be there in a minute."

Lila slipped inside the house.

Emma Cate tugged at his hand. "Come on, Daddy Sam. We're going to miss Hunter putting de star on de tree. It's a very special job."

He crouched beside her. "I want to talk with you about something important."

Where to begin? He swallowed. *Help me, God. Help me undo the damage I never meant to cause. Show me what I should say.*

"I love you, Emma Cate."

Smiling, she captured his face between her hands. "I love you, Daddy Sam. Can we go? De star is de last, most important ding."

"Not just yet."

She shivered.

"You shouldn't have come out here without a coat." Sitting on the cold wooden plank, he opened his jacket. Drawing her into his lap, he wrapped his coat around her. "I know you don't remember, but before me, you had another daddy and mommy."

Her smile about broke his heart. "My udder mommy and daddy are in heaven."

Sam hugged her close. "Yes, they are."

"But…" She shook her finger at him.

He fought a smile. Emma Cate had definitely been spending way too much time with Miss IdaLee. "But what, baby doll?"

"But…" She touched the tip of her finger to his chin to ensure she had his full attention.

Yep, way too much time with Miss IdaLee.

"God knew you needed me, so He sent me to you." Her eyes lit up. "'Cause He knew you needed a little girl for your very own."

A tear rolled down his cheek. "Yes, I do."

She caught the tear before it fell off his jaw. "Silly Daddy Sam."

He fought past the lump in his throat. "So you know what that means, Emma Cate?"

She tilted her small head. "What?"

"That you are my daughter. And I think you should call me Daddy from now on."

Her brow scrunched.

"Because I'm going to love you forever, Emma Cate. And you don't have to worry about me ever leaving you."

Like his father had.

Her rosebud mouth pursed. "Not call you Daddy Sam?"

"Would you like that, to call me Daddy?" His voice sounded hoarse.

Her smile warmed places inside his heart that had been numb since the day he came home from school and found his father gone.

"Of course I would." She patted his bristly cheek. "'Cause dat's what daughters call dere daddies, right?"

He could no longer control the tears welling in his eyes. "That's right."

She threw her arms around him, and he hugged her tight.

Placing her small palms on his shirt, she pushed back. "So Daddy?"

He swiped at his eyes. "Yes, baby doll?"

She eased off his lap. "We need to get in dere and see Hunter put dat star on de tree, okay?"

"Okay." He allowed her to lug him upright.

Inside, they found IdaLee's family gathered around the tree in the front parlor. The old woman sat ensconced on a small armchair, looking on as the rest of them put the finishing touches on the tree.

Cliff Penry flashed them a smile. "Time for the star." He handed a silver-gilded, five-pointed star to Hunter.

The little boy held it out to Emma Cate. "Youngest is supposed to put it on the tree."

Sam's niece—no—his daughter's eyes grew large.

Hunter nudged the star at Emma Cate. "This year that's you."

"Me?" Her eyes flitted to Sam as if seeking permission.

He rubbed his neck. "I don't know—"

"That's our tradition." Miss IdaLee raised her chin. "Lift her up there, Samuel, so she can reach."

A smile broke out across Emma Cate's face. "I can't believe Hunter picked me." She tugged at Sam's sleeve. "Putting on de star is a very, very, very important job."

He flicked his eyes at Lila, who smiled. "So I hear."

Emma Cate did a tiny dance of sheer happiness. "Dank you. Dank you, Hunter." She threw her arms around the mini cowboy.

From the pained expression on his face, Sam reckoned girls hadn't yet made it to Hunter's favorites list. Which, as a daddy, cheered him to no end.

Hunter freed himself from her exuberant embrace. "I can still flip the light switch, though, right, Mom?"

AnnaBeth laughed. "I think that can be arranged."

Grabbing hold of Emma Cate, Sam hoisted her onto his shoulders. "Hang on."

Stretching, she fitted the base of the star over the lone branch sticking up at the top. He connected the plug to the dangling extension cord hidden beneath the branches.

"Get ready!" Hunter put a hand on the light switch. "One...two...three..." He flicked the toggle.

Multiple strands of lights sprang to life. And at the top of the tree, the star glowed.

"Hurray!" Hunter fist-pumped. "Christmas has begun."

Everyone clapped. Sam lowered Emma Cate from her perch.

Her eyes shone. "It's going to be de best Christmas ever, Daddy."

Sam caught Lila's eye. Something almost visceral passed between them.

This special day. His deeper relationship with Emma Cate. All thanks to Lila.

"Yes." He finally managed to force the words around the emotion he was feeling. "I think it will."

Chapter Six

By now, Sam had expected to hear back about his bid on the Asheville development, but there was still no word.

In his experience, no news didn't always mean good news. In fact, usually the opposite.

He didn't have time to brood, though. It would be a short, three-day workweek for him. He had to take Emma Cate to her out-of-state grandparents' on Thursday.

Sam was glad she'd get the opportunity to spend time with them. In a few years, it wouldn't be so easy for her to miss an entire week of instruction. The older she became, it would be harder to justify taking her out of school.

This year, he wouldn't even get the chance to spend the night with her at the farm. It would be all he could do to drive back from Virginia and be ready Friday morning to leave with Lila for the wedding.

A jam-packed week.

On Monday, he and the crew began an interior project for the Truelove library renovation. It was their first local government contract. Becoming one of the county government's preferred vendors had involved tons of red tape. He hoped this job would be the first of many government projects for Paint by the Numbers.

It hadn't yet snowed, but the weather in Truelove had taken a decided turn toward the frosty end of the thermometer.

Due to both their busy schedules, over the next few days, he didn't see much of Lila, although Emma Cate continued to keep him informed about Miss Penry's wardrobe.

He and Lila did exchange texts. But texts weren't the same as talking in person. Two weeks ago, he and Lila had barely known one another.

Midway through the week, with no small measure of disquiet, he realized he missed talking to her on a daily basis. When he considered how quickly he'd grown used to seeing her every day—looked forward to, counted on it, even—he felt more than slightly concerned.

On Friday morning, he pulled up in front of her house. She must have been watching for him. By the time he got out of the truck, she was already on the porch with her suitcase, locking the door behind her.

He took the steps two at a time. "Lila."

She tucked the key into her purse. "Sam."

He grinned. She grinned back.

Sam reached for her suitcase.

"I can get that."

He shook his head. "As your date for the weekend, luggage falls within my purview."

She pursed her lips. "You're my plus-one for the weekend. But thank you."

Lila had assured him all pre-wedding activities were casual, so like her, he'd worn jeans and a cable-knit sweater. Her jeans were upturned just above her suede ankle boots. Over her ivory-colored sweater she wore a wool, cape-shawl thingy in a color that reminded him of apricots.

He offered his arm.

She raised her eyebrow. "Another one of your duties? We're not even at the resort yet."

To his way of thinking, not so much a duty as a pleasure, but he figured he'd spook her if he admitted that.

"Practice makes perfect." He winked. "And I wouldn't want you to turn an ankle in those fancy high-heel boots of yours."

"They're not that high." She stretched her foot out in front of her, as if examining the boots for the first time. "But you're right. Better safe than sorry." She tucked her hand into the crook of his elbow. "One of your bigger jobs this weekend. Don't let me make a fool out of myself."

After Sam put her suitcase behind the seat in the truck cab, they soon left Truelove behind. The wedding was being held at one of the premier winter destination resorts in the Blue Ridge, a couple of hours north.

"I checked the forecast this morning." As the truck steadily climbed the mountain passes, he scanned the bare tree branches lining the highway. "The higher elevations got the snow Truelove didn't get."

"Paige will get her wish for a snowy white wedding." Lila shifted on the seat. "Was Emma Cate all right when you left her at her grandparents' yesterday?"

"Surprisingly, yes." He shot her a quick look. "Thanks to your insight. Since Emma Cate and I talked on Thanksgiving, she's been less clingy when I took her to school this week."

Lila nodded. "I noticed she seems more at ease when she's not with you."

"I wish I could say the same for me."

"Was it hard saying goodbye to her yesterday?"

"Very." He blew out a breath. "And it gets harder every time. Kind of caught me off guard."

"Does Emma Cate spend much time with her paternal grandparents?"

"A week in summer. A week around the holidays." He gave her a sheepish smile. "About all my heart can take, but I make an effort to help her remain connected to her father's people. They're farmers. Not wealthy. She talks with them weekly on the phone."

"But you don't share custody?"

He shook his head. "They are a lot older than my mom. That's why when Emma Cate was born, my sister asked me to be her guardian in the unlikely event something happened. I never dreamed both of Emma Cate's parents would be killed in a car accident before she reached her second birthday."

"Was Emma Cate in the car when it happened?"

"Strapped in her car seat. A rain-slick highway. An SUV was going too fast and hydroplaned. Hit their vehicle head-on."

Lila's face clouded. "I'm so sorry, Sam."

He tightened his grip on the wheel. "My sister and her husband were killed on impact. When first responders arrived, Emma Cate was crying, but she'd suffered no injuries." He cleared his throat. "But enough sad memories."

"Does Emma Cate enjoy spending time with her grandparents?"

"She's probably having the time of her life." He gave Lila a wry smile. "They spoil her rotten. Lots of ice cream. Late bedtimes. She gets to feed the animals on the farm, too."

"Emma Cate will miss you, though."

He already missed the feel of her little arms around his neck. "I'll call her every day." He laughed. "When I can catch her between farmyard fun."

The truck ate up the miles. They continued to chat and laugh. The time flew by. Lila was easy to talk to.

Sam had always believed he and Lila came from two separate, unable-to-be-breached worlds. But they actually had a lot in common. They liked the same movies. Same kind of music.

However, she was more of a reader than him. If he got still for more than five minutes, he tended to fall asleep.

She told him about the projects she was working on. He told her about their current project at the Truelove library and about the prospective big opportunity in Asheville.

Her eyes widened. "I didn't think about how you'd have to miss work."

"My crew can survive without me for a weekend." He steered around a curve on the winding mountain road. "My mom's been telling me I needed to get away and do something fun that doesn't involve a four-year-old."

"To tell you the truth, I've been dreading the wedding." Lila took a deep breath. "Until you agreed to go with me." She smiled. "It will be fun, won't it?"

Something in his chest eased. She was right. The weekend promised to be full of fun. Mainly because he'd be spending it with her.

Along with sixty of Paige Lindstrom's other nearest and dearest.

"I was surprised when you told me you were Paige's maid of honor. I didn't realize you and Paige were…" He searched for the right word. "…close."

"We were best friends when we were Emma Cate's age. But Paige was always athletic and bubbly. I wasn't. And later, she found other friends." She knotted her fingers in her lap. "The whole popularity scene wasn't my thing. We ran in different circles. We drifted apart…" Her voice dropped.

He cut his eyes at her. And though she didn't say it, he could imagine how hurt the younger Lila must have been by her so-called friend's desertion.

From what he remembered of high school, Paige had been caught up with her cheerleader friends and, in his opinion, her own self-importance. Especially after she was crowned home-coming queen their senior year.

Lila turned toward him. "Paige was really popular, like you."

"I wouldn't call myself popular."

"You were on the football team. A game-winning quarterback. Of course you were popular." She threw him a funny-strange sort of smile. "With lots of girlfriends."

He scowled. "I didn't have girlfriends. I had dates."

"Lots of dates, as I recall."

Sam fidgeted. "They only liked me because I played football. Because of my dad, they thought I was a bad-boy jock, and they wanted to use me to annoy their parents. I wasn't interested in them."

He'd wanted to live down his father's reputation, not add to it.

She shrugged. "They were sure interested in you, though."

Maybe so, although he was just beginning to realize the only girl who wasn't into him was the only girl who might have mattered.

She sighed. "I'm not looking forward to spending the weekend with Paige's cheerleader friends."

Why had Lila agreed to be her maid of honor in the first place? It didn't make any sense to him.

"But maybe it won't be so bad." She put on a smile. "We've all grown up since then."

"Those girls were always jealous of you."

Her eyes widened. "Of me? Why?"

"You've got more talent in your little finger than those women possess in their entire bodies."

"Thank you, Sam." From the small smile teasing the corners of her lips, he could tell his words had pleased her.

"How did you and Paige reconnect?"

"You know that her parents moved to Asheville after we graduated, right?"

He nodded.

"For a while, Paige lost her way."

He looked at Lila. "What do you mean?"

"After high school, I didn't hear from Paige for several years, until one night she called me out of the blue. She was a mess on the phone. I could barely understand her for the sobbing."

"What was wrong? What had happened?"

Lila looked troubled. "She'd become bulimic and was suicidal."

Bulimic? Paige had always been rail thin.

"At that point, Paige didn't want anyone to know. She called me because she said I was the only one she could trust who liked her for herself."

"What did you do?"

"I drove from my school to her university

dorm. I took her home to her parents, and together we told them about her struggles. She was in therapy for a long time, but she's doing well now. She shares her experience with other teenagers, hoping they will learn from what she went through."

"You were a very good friend."

Better than Paige Lindstrom deserved. But Lila's loyalty was one of the qualities he most admired about her.

"Paige never returned to the university. She got her paralegal license and works for her father's law firm."

"Is that where she met her future husband?"

"N-no…"

At the hitch in her voice, he glanced over. She'd ducked her head so he couldn't see her face. He didn't like not being able to see her face.

"Lila?"

"Tristan is an architect. We met at the School of Design. He and I…" She pinched her lips together.

"You and he what?" he grunted.

"We dated."

He stared at her. "You and Paige's groom dated. For how long?"

Flushing, she twisted a lock of hair around her finger. "Almost a year."

"Was it serious?"

"I thought so. He came home with me on fall break. Tristan and Paige met when she drove up from Asheville to visit, and the rest is history."

Reaching over, he took hold of her hand. "I'm sorry."

"For them, it was love at first sight."

He grimaced. "But for her to ask you to be her maid of honor…"

"Paige doesn't know about my feelings for him. I guess he saw me more as an art school buddy, not as a girlfriend."

Doesn't know? Her feelings. *Present tense?*

His chest tightened. Did she still have feelings for Tristan?

The truck crested the hill. Below them, the majestic, historic white-columned inn nestled in the sweep of a snow-covered valley. He followed the signs to guest parking.

"Wow." Lila's eyes shone. "I've never been here before."

Nor had he. The resort's clientele weren't exactly the kind of people the Gibsons rubbed shoulders with. His stomach clenched. He didn't want to embarrass Lila. He didn't want her to regret asking him to come.

"Don't get out yet." Jumping out of the cab, he hurried around to the passenger side. He flung open the door and helped her descend from the crew cab. "Careful. Watch your footing."

He retrieved her suitcase and his duffel. They followed the sidewalk to the imposing front entrance. Inside the lobby, an ornate chandelier glittered above their heads.

Expensive oriental carpets lay scattered around the white marble floor. Clustered on the formal, silk-covered chairs and sofas, various groupings of guests conversed in low voices.

At the registration desk, a middle-aged woman in a navy-blue suit keyed in their names. "You're with the Lindstrom-Becker wedding party, correct?"

Lila adjusted the strap of her purse on her shoulder. "That's right."

The woman handed them two key cards. "Miss Penry, you will find your room on the second floor with the rest of the bridal party. Mr. Gibson, your room is on the third floor." She gave them instructions about finding the elevator. "The bridal couple have thoughtfully prepared welcome goodies in your rooms. You will also find the weekend itinerary in the basket as well."

Calling Lila's name, her arms outstretched, Paige Lindstrom swept toward them. She was pretty much as he recalled her. American Girl Doll pretty, with dark brown eyes and long, straight blond hair.

She wore a baby-blue sweater and black jeans tucked into tall black boots, which he guessed were expensive. Paige engulfed Lila in an embrace. "It's so wonderful to see you."

A wave of exotic perfume overwhelmed his senses. He crinkled his nose.

"Oh. Hi, Sam." Letting go of Lila, she stepped back. "I couldn't believe it when I heard you were Lila's plus-one."

He stiffened. "Why's that?"

Paige blinked at him. "I… I didn't know you two knew each other."

"We went to high school together." He frowned. "Of course Lila and I know one another."

He was really glad he'd come. Lila was far too openhearted and perhaps too quick to trust. The jury was still out in his mind on Paige's motivations. If Paige Lindstrom believed she and her mean-girl cohorts could bully Lila, she had another thought coming.

"I only meant—"

"We're friends." He narrowed his gaze. "We hang out."

Lila shot him a look. But it was true. They did hang out—at the paint store, at church, on Thanksgiving. At least, they had while he was painting her house.

A young man about their age headed across the lobby toward them. Paige's face transformed. "Tristan, darling. Look who's arrived."

Not quite as tall as Sam, Paige's fiancé was slim with dark brown eyes. A lock of dark brown hair flopped across his broad forehead.

Behind brown tortoiseshell glasses, the man's brown eyes gleamed. "It's so wonderful to see you again." He smiled at Lila.

The expression in her eyes became unreadable.

Sam's heart fell. Was Tristan the real reason Lila had agreed to act as maid of honor? Was she still hung up on him?

"I'm Sam Gibson." He stepped between them. "Lila's date." He thrust out his hand.

Paige's fiancé shook his hand. "Tristan Becker." He eyed Sam, sizing him up. "You're with Lila?"

Her eyes darted between them. "Actually—"

"Yes, I'm with Lila." Squeezing Tristan's hand till Paige's fiancé winced, he bared his teeth. "You and I are both blessed with two lovely women, way out of our league."

"I didn't mean—" Tristan jerked his hand free. "Uh, yes, we are." He pushed his glasses up the bridge of his nose.

Lila took his arm. "Sam?"

He broadened his shoulders. "We were going to our rooms."

"Perfect." Paige gave them a brilliant smile. "You're just in time for our first wedding party activity. A snowman-building contest out on the lawn."

Lila looked at her watch. "What time should we be there?"

"We'll start in about thirty minutes. Get settled and then come join us. We're pairing off into teams. As creative as you are, I can't wait to see what you come up with." Paige gave her another hug. "I am so, so happy you're here to share my special day with me."

Tristan caught Lila's hand. And Sam went rigid. "It's so good to see you. It's been too long."

Whose fault was that?

He seethed. "We should go, Lila." On the pretext of moving toward the elevator, he removed her hand from Becker's limp grasp.

She glowered at him, but she allowed him to pull her away.

Although if Paige and Tristan hadn't met, this weekend could very well have been Lila and Tristan's wedding. That idea nearly stopped him cold. *Absolutely not. Would've never happened.*

She had too much good sense. What had she ever seen in a sop like Becker? Though Tristan's loss was hands down his gain.

Just shy of the elevator, he ground to a halt. *Seriously?* Where had that come from?

"What?"

Distracted, he rubbed the back of his neck. "Nothing."

"What's going on with you?" Waiting for the elevator, she motioned toward the lobby. "You were rude to Tristan."

"Not a fan." He jabbed the button again. "He's an idiot."

She glared at him. "I'm surprised at you. You don't even know him."

"I know enough."

The elevator whooshed open.

His lips twisted. "I'm surprised at how friendly you were to a man who hurt you." He stepped inside.

Clutching her purse strap, she followed him. "I forgave him for not loving me, Sam."

He punched the numbers on the panel for their floors. "Like I said, he's an idiot."

She cut her gaze at him, but he clamped his lips together. The doors slid shut.

As the elevator rose, shoulder to shoulder they stared unspeaking as the numbers ticked by. Christmas music played softly in the background. Reaching the second floor, the elevator dinged.

He took hold of her suitcase. "I'll wheel this to your room."

"That's not necess—"

"I intend to make sure you get there safely."

The doors opened. "I'll collect you for the snow-man contest."

Standing across the gap, he braced his shoulders against the door, holding it for her to exit. "Twenty minutes."

The doors closed behind them.

She tilted her head. "I don't know if I've said it enough, but thank you for coming with me."

His eyes locked onto hers.

For one dizzying second, he forgot everything. Except for her and him, standing outside the elevator on the plush crimson carpet.

Taking a steadying breath, he held up his palm. "Team Gibry." He smirked.

Her lips curved. "You mean Team Penson."

"Don't leave me hanging, Penry."

Laughing, she high-fived him. The touch of her hand against his skin sent a tingle down the length of his arm. He swallowed.

He decided then and there to make it the best weekend she'd ever had. And maybe, it might just end up being the best weekend of his life, too.

Sam Gibson was a man of his word. In exactly twenty minutes, he knocked on Lila's door. Tucking a lavender knit cap over her hair, she hurried to let him inside.

"I'm ready." She flung open the door.

When his eyes lit up, her heart kicked up a notch.

"I like your hat." Using the tip of his finger, he set the pom-pom on the top of her cap in motion. "Got your gloves?"

She nodded, but lest he somehow read her thoughts, she lowered her gaze and concentrated on winding the matching scarf around her throat.

He'd donned a heavier Carhartt coat and a blue cap that matched his eyes. When he helped her slip into her puffy black coat, her pulse leaped. He smelled amazing. A scrumptious blend of woodsy notes and soap.

She reached for a small, plastic bag on the bed. "What's that?"

"Paige gave the wedding party a heads-up on pre-wedding activities." She let him take a peek inside the bag. "My secret weapon for the snowman contest."

In the elevator, he nudged her shoulder. "Go Team Penson."

She smiled.

All the way to the lobby, they talked strategy. The doorman ushered them outside. Twenty people from the little flower girl to Tristan's elderly grandparents had assembled on the snowy front lawn.

Paige's elegant mother swept toward them. "How wonderful to see you again, dear."

Lila introduced Sam to Mrs. Lindstrom and to Paige's patrician, silver-haired father.

Paige clapped her gloves together to get everyone's attention. "I want to welcome everyone. Tristan and I are so happy you will be part of our special day." She took the opportunity to introduce the wedding party to one another.

The groomsmen were Tristan's friends from college and a few men with whom he now worked. Lila already knew the bridesmaids—Paige's sister and a cousin. Two of the other women had cheered with Paige in high school—Courtney and Madison.

Last month at Paige's bridal shower in Asheville, she'd made it her business to keep her distance from those two. But when their paths had crossed, Courtney and Madison were cordial enough. Maybe everyone *had* matured into nicer human beings.

"I think everyone has already selected their partners for the snowman contest." Paige surveyed the gathering. "You will have two hours to create your work of art."

"To create the coolest snowman ever." Tristan slipped an arm around Paige's waist. "Cool? Get it?"

Several people tittered at his pun. She smiled. Sam curled his lip.

Paige gave her fiancé a fond look. "Teams will

need to work together. Make your snowman tall, traditional or just plain silly. When time's up, the resort staff will cast their votes and declare the winner."

"Do your best." Tristan winked at his soon-to-be bride. "But be warned, as y'all know, we make a pretty awesome team already."

Sam made a sound low in his throat. Like gagging. Lila cut her eyes at him.

"It's not about the competition. It's just for fun," she whispered.

He leaned closer. "Don't kid yourself." The warmth of his breath tickled her earlobe. "Life is a competition. A competition Team Penson is going to win."

The teams went to work. Fluffy but not too dry, the snow was perfect for building snowmen. The hotel had provided essential building tools, like snow shovels and small buckets.

Additional items for outfitting their creations also lay within easy reach—charcoal, big black buttons and carrots for those aiming for more iconic snowman features. There was an assortment of branches for arms. Various art supplies like markers, glue, glitter and cardboard rounded out the possibilities.

"Structure is key." Sam scooped a large glob of snow and packed it in his gloved hands. "For stability, we should aim for a three-two-one ratio."

Lila held in a grin.

Their school had won the area football conference title every year they were in high school. In their senior year, the football team had played for the state championship. Thanks in large part to Sam Gibson. She should've known he'd be competitive.

Rolling the snowballs on the ground to achieve the desired size, he focused on creating the bottom ball. She worked on the middle one.

He packed extra snow around the base of the bottom ball. "Gotta brace it."

She stuck her tongue in her cheek. "I didn't say anything."

He tugged the ends of her scarf. "But I could see the question in your eyes."

She made a mock bow. "I defer to your obvious expertise."

He leveled off the top of the bottom snowball. "Flattening the top before placing the next ball on top provides—"

"Let me guess." She fluttered her lashes at him. "More stability."

He hefted the medium-size ball and put it in place. "You're catching on, Penry. I'll make a master snowman builder out of you yet." He threw her a lopsided grin.

And her knees almost gave out underneath her. "Now for the head."

He didn't seem to notice the effect he had on her. *Just as well.* While he worked on the snowman's face, she rummaged through the scarves she'd brought with her to the wedding.

"That gives me an idea. Hold on a sec. I've got something in my truck that will complete the look." He soon returned with a small painter's brush.

Lila cut an oblong shape out of a piece of cardboard she found on the table. Utilizing the markers, she created an artist's paint palette. He added a couple of branch appendages. And she positioned the art palette within the fork of one of the arms.

The hotel photographer took a picture of each team behind their snow person. The staff had set up tables around the lawn with crocks of steaming apple cider and hot chocolate with marshmallows to warm the wedding party.

She stood back to admire their handiwork and to check out their competition. "Think we'll win?"

Munching on a powdered snowball cookie, he cocked his head. "Don't you?"

In the end, every team won a category. The youngest members of the wedding party won Best Superhero Snowman. A team of groomsmen won Biggest Snowman. The cheerleader bridesmaids won Best Snowwoman. Paige and Tristan won Best Traditional.

Lila took a sip of the spiced apple cider.

"So lame." Sam brushed his mouth against the cap at her ear. "No imagination. Figures."

Lila sputtered. "Behave," she whispered.

When the judges declared their snow artist—Best Creative Use of Accessories, he mouthed *I told you so.*

In keeping with the winter wonderland theme, cold-themed prizes were awarded to the winners. Paige's parents did the honors. The prizes included tickets to a Carolina Hurricanes hockey game in Raleigh and gift certificates for frozen yogurt.

She and Sam won passes to an Asheville ice-skating rink. Walking across the snowy lawn to the lodge, she pressed them in his hand.

He shook his head. "The tickets belong to both of us."

"Emma Cate will love these. Take her when she gets home."

"Here's a better idea." He tucked one of the passes into her coat pocket. "Emma Cate would love to go ice skating with her favorite teacher."

"Ahh…" Lila's eyes watered. "I'm her favorite teacher?"

"I'll buy Emma Cate a ticket, too. The three

of us can go to Asheville and make a day of it. What do you think?"

She thought it a marvelous plan. "Sounds great."

He grinned. "It's a date, then."

But by the new year, she could be headed to California. Only two more weeks to go before she'd hear if she'd won the art-residency position.

Other than telling AnnaBeth, she wanted to keep her artist-in-residence application a secret until it was a done deal. And why she'd put off telling her parents about her future plans and dreams until she absolutely had to. She was such a people pleaser, usually to her own detriment.

Her enthusiasm for the position dimming, a lump settled in her throat. *What's wrong with me?*

She'd worked for years to achieve her dream. She ought to be ecstatic at the thought of possibly beginning a brand-new life.

But the idea of a continent between her, Sam and Emma Cate suddenly made Lila want to weep.

Chapter Seven

After the snowman contest, she and Sam retreated to their rooms to get ready for the wedding rehearsal.

She pulled out the outfit she planned to wear tonight. AnnaBeth's mother had helped her put it together. First thing on the day after Thanksgiving, AnnaBeth and her mom had arrived at her house.

Victoria had wanted to take a look at her closet to get a sense of her style. Then they'd headed out to the larger city of Asheville. Shopping with AnnaBeth and her mom had been fun.

Utilizing most of what Lila already had in her wardrobe, Victoria had helped her buy the one showpiece item that brought her outfit for the rehearsal evening together.

Very feminine. With a touch of whimsy. She loved how she felt wearing it. She hoped Sam would like her in it, too.

Hearing a soft knock, she opened the door to find Paige standing outside in the hallway.

"Oh. Hi." Lila peered at Paige. "Is everything okay?"

Usually the epitome of perfection, Paige's blond hair was mussed, and her face was blotchy. Her eyes brimming, Paige clamped her lips together, unable to speak.

Catching hold of her friend's hand, she pulled the bride into the room. "What is it?"

"Can we talk?" Paige's lips wobbled. "Just for a minute? There's something I needed to say to you."

Unsure where this was headed, she drew Paige toward the green silk armchairs near the window overlooking the front lawn.

The late-afternoon sun lent a shimmery glint to the snow people below. The lavender shadows cast by the overhanging ridge of mountains surrounding the hotel lengthened.

"I didn't know if I'd get another chance this weekend, so I decided to come find you." Perched on the edge of the cushion, Paige crumpled a tissue in her hand. "I wanted to thank you and tell you how much your friendship has meant to me over the years."

Lila sank into the opposite chair. What had happened since they parted on the lawn to reduce Paige to tears?

"I know I haven't always been a good friend to you."

She made a motion of protest, but Paige held up her hand.

"It's true. I was thinking over everything we've shared. You gave me back my life."

Lila shook her head.

"Yes. You did. If you hadn't dropped everything that night when I called…" Tears rolled down Paige's cheeks. "I don't know where I would be right now. Or if I would be alive. I certainly wouldn't be here. As for Tristan and me…" She turned her face toward the window.

Had something happened with Tristan? Lila hoped not. She'd also long ago gotten over him. Since getting to know Sam, she'd realized she and Tristan didn't have much in common. They wouldn't have suited each other. But he and Paige were perfect together.

"You're the best friend I've ever had. I'm aware I can be self-absorbed." With the tissue, Paige dabbed the moisture on her face. "I haven't asked about you and Sam. It shows how out of touch I've been that I had no idea you were seeing each other."

"Sam and I…" She fidgeted. "We're…"

Did she really want to admit he was only here as her plus-one because they'd made a deal for the wedding?

Paige gave her a small smile. "You and Sam are good together."

She knew that for Sam this weekend was a business arrangement. But she was terribly afraid somewhere along the line it had stopped being that for her.

Dropping her gaze, she fingered the gold fringe of the armchair pillow. "We're only friends."

"Oh, really?" Laughing softly, Paige arched her eyebrow. "I see how he looks at you, and friendship doesn't cover it by half."

She felt her face flame. Sam looked at her? It couldn't be true. Not in the way Paige implied.

"There's definitely a spark between you." Paige crossed her ankles and tucked them underneath the chair. "Trust me, I know about these things. And I've never seen you so...so..."

"So what?"

"Glowing. Radiant." Paige lifted her chin. "Or as happy. As for Sam? The Sam Gibson I remember had a chip on his shoulder a mile high and a mile wide. But he seems more at ease when he's with you. He's definitely into you, Lila."

She couldn't have been more shocked.

If only it was true. And if it was? What about California? Her mouth went dry. A relationship with Sam was a complication she'd hadn't foreseen.

Neither Sam nor Truelove fit anywhere into

her future plans. The fact she'd started to second-guess those plans troubled her. She didn't belong in Truelove, and Sam wasn't leaving.

Paige chuckled. "I also remember how you crushed on him all through high school."

She groaned. "And how totally oblivious he was to my charms. Such as they were."

Paige's lips quirked. "From what I've observed today, not so oblivious now."

She'd always believed love wasn't in her future. And if it was, that she would find it with someone from her yet-to-be-claimed art-loving tribe. Like in California.

Yet was Paige right? Could there be something growing between Sam and her? Something worth sticking around for?

"I want you to find your happily-ever-after, too." Paige's mouth trembled. "Your own true love. The way Tristan and I…" She knotted the tissue between her fingers. "I—I don't know why I'm so emotional."

Lila raised her brow into a question mark. "Maybe because you're getting married tomorrow?"

Through her tears, Paige gave her a wan smile. "There is that."

Reaching over, Lila patted her hand. "I imagine it's wonderful and overwhelming all at the same time. Marrying the man you love. A dream come true."

"It is." Paige sighed. "But I've been so busy getting ready for the wedding."

"And probably not taking care of yourself like you should." Lila lowered her voice. "Are you all right?"

"I'm not purging, if that's what you mean." Paige straightened. "I'm merely tired. And anxious for everything to go well."

Suddenly, it occurred to Lila how exhausting it would have been to be Paige. The all-consuming effort and energy it would take to maintain such physical perfection. The crushing pressure to maintain expectations, both external and self-imposed.

Leaving Lila with no time for the things she truly cared about, like spending time with the people she loved.

No time to nurture her sweet little art protegés at school and help them blossom. No time for the beauty of the world to fill her senses so that she was compelled to put paint to canvas.

And for the first time in their friendship, she was glad God had made her just as she was.

She slipped to her knees in front of Paige's chair. "The only thing that matters is that twenty-four hours from now you will be Mrs. Tristan Becker. Everything else?" She fluttered her hand. "Icing on the wedding cake."

Paige smiled. A real smile this time. "So you're saying I need to put things in perspective."

"You expect too much of yourself. Relax. This is your weekend. You're surrounded by the people who love you. Don't get so caught up in unimportant details that you lose the joy of this moment."

Paige sucked in a breath. "You're right. It was the drive for unrealistic perfection that got me in trouble in college." She exhaled. "Once again, you've talked me off the ledge, dear friend."

Lila got to her feet. "Glad to help. Comes with the maid-of-honor package."

Paige rose, too. "Speaking of maid-of-honor duties, there's something I need to ask you."

"Okay…"

"Will you stand in for me at the rehearsal?"

Lila frowned. "What?"

"I don't want Tristan to watch me walk down the aisle at the rehearsal." Paige teared again. "I want to save that special moment when he looks at me for the day of our wedding."

Lila fought to keep her dismay off her features. Stand-in brides at the wedding rehearsal were a tradition in the South.

"I'm not sure I'd be the best—"

"Oh, will you, Lila? Please say yes."

It was an honor to be asked, but how could she graciously extricate herself and decline?

Paige clasped her hand. "I'll be right there in the background, observing. Getting the visual layout from the guests' perspective." She smiled. "It always comes back to perspective, doesn't it?"

Walking down the aisle toward Tristan promised to be awkward and uncomfortable. Yet how could she refuse? Paige might have her issues with perfection, but Lila was well aware she had her own issues with saying no.

Although the upside of her inability to say no to becoming Paige's maid of honor was that it had brought her to this weekend with Sam. The man of her girlhood dreams. A dream come true.

Was it possible to have more than one dream? Lila bit her lip. Why was her life so complicated?

Because you're such an emotional dilly-dallier, that's why.

Not a kind, helpful or useful thought. But true? *The truth hurts, Frizzy Hair.*

Lila clenched her teeth.

Sometimes—actually more than sometimes— she wished she could just smack the mean girl upside her straight, brown, perfectly coiffed head.

"Fine." She shrugged. "I'll be your proxy bride for the rehearsal."

Paige hugged her. "Fabulous. It'll be good practice for when you're the bride for real."

She rolled her eyes. "Like that's ever going to happen."

"Don't be so sure. I think Sam Gibson's got a thing for redheads." Paige smirked. "Artsy redheads."

Sam rode down the elevator with Lila. "You're sure I don't need a coat and tie for the rehearsal?"

"Paige said it's casual. She wanted the dinner to have a cozier feel. Pizza around the fireplace. And later, s'mores." She looked at him. "Jeans and sweaters are just right."

The elevator opened, and they walked across the lobby.

He held the door for her to exit through the front entrance. "You're not wearing jeans."

"I decided to wear leggings with the tunic and boots."

A tunic. Was that what they called the knee-length jumper she had on? Women and their clothes. So complicated. So much to learn.

He'd never heard of a scrunchie until Emma Cate came into his life. And adolescence promised all kinds of less-than-pleasant surprises he'd have to add to his bank of knowledge.

Outside on the sidewalk, he gave Lila an admiring glance. She'd thrown a black-and-tan-plaid shawl around her shoulders. The ivory lace top underneath the brown corduroy tunic matched her ivory lace leggings. The laced-up, brown leather ankle boots reminded him of a television show he used to watch as a kid about pioneers.

So quirky. So dare-to-be-herself. So wonderfully Lila.

He offered his arm. She took it. They followed the paved path around the side of the hotel and through a snow-daubed glade of evergreen trees lit by strings of fairy lights.

The small stone chapel lay around the bend. Lights glowed through the stained-glass windows, spilling colorful reflections on the snow.

"It's so lovely," she gasped.

His gaze darted to her. "Yes. Very lovely." And he wasn't necessarily thinking of the chapel.

But the setting *was* very picturesque. And in present company, very romantic. For once, the idea of beginning a relationship with someone didn't disturb him. Not if the woman was Lila.

A smile curving her lips, she tucked a wispy curl behind her ear. And his heart did that funny rat-tat-tat-tat thing it did when he thought about her hair.

For tonight's occasion, she'd put her hair in a bun on top of her head. But he preferred her hair long, with billowing waves of curls skimming her shoulders. He stumbled.

She threw him a curious look. He gave her a

reassuring, if weak, smile. Had he lost his mind? Since when did he have a preference for the way she wore her hair?

They joined the rest of the bridal party inside the chapel. Wooden beams soared overhead. Pews bracketed either side of the red-carpeted aisle. At the front altar, Paige and Tristan were in deep conversation with the hotel wedding co-ordinator.

Sam didn't know any of the other men, but he recognized two of the bridesmaids from True-love. They'd been part of the crowd he'd hung with in high school, comprised of athletes and cheerleaders.

The woman with long, straight brown hair waved. Lila stiffened. The two women made a beeline for them. He didn't remember either of their names.

"Sam Gibson," the petite blonde gushed.

The brunette slid her hand into the crook of his elbow. "Remember when you were my escort at homecoming?"

Lila slipped her hand off his arm.

He remembered, all right. Along with the rest of the football team, he'd been roped into escort-ing the homecoming court. In his opinion, he'd drawn the short straw with the catty brunette.

"And you two made such a cute couple at the dance later," the blonde chimed in.

Both of them ignored Lila as if she wasn't even standing there.

Sam frowned. "I'm sure you both remember Lila Penry from our class at school."

He reached to touch the small of her back. But with an inscrutable look on her face, she moved an arm's length away, inserting distance between them instead. And he felt the loss of more than her physical presence.

"Oh yeah." The brunette shrugged. "We saw her at the bridal shower."

The blonde took hold of his arm. The brunette took hold of the other one. Not that Lila noticed or seemed to care. Angling, she scanned the crowd inside the church as if searching for someone.

She probably thought he'd lied to her about not having lots of girlfriends. And if she believed these two were indicative of his girlfriends, probably questioning his taste in women in general.

Did she imagine he would be interested in them? Nothing could be further from the truth. He hadn't cared for their type in high school, and they certainly weren't his type now, either.

It struck him that of all the single women in Truelove, the matchmakers had never seen fit to try to set him up with these two. Maybe the old women had more insight than he'd credited them with. Or perhaps they knew him better than he'd supposed.

Sam remembered the brunette's name. Courtney Askew. And he also remembered how miserable he'd been the night of homecoming. How he couldn't wait for the date to end.

He was wondering who Lila had gone to the homecoming dance with—or if she'd gone at all—when she moved away, abandoning him to the clutches of the cheerleaders.

Unlike Tristan Becker, he wasn't the kind of guy to go from one girl to the other. Sam was exactly where he wanted to be—with Lila. And her seemingly low opinion of his character bothered him more than it ought to.

Lila joined Paige near the altar.

Grimacing, he freed himself from Courtney and the blonde. Tuning out their self-absorbed account of what they'd been doing since high school. Each of them trying to outvie the other. His conversational contribution was neither solicited nor necessary.

Which was fine by him. He only had eyes for Lila. When she smiled at something one of the groomsmen said, something sour churned in his belly.

The groomsmen were engineers. A lawyer. A doctor. And what was he?

A paint contractor. Honest work, but compared

to those guys? He was nobody special. And Lila deserved special.

Tristan's groomsmen had college degrees. *Like Lila.* They had great careers ahead of them. *Like Lila.* From respectable families. *Like Lila.*

As for him?

He was the son of a con man. A struggling single parent, he worked with his hands. Compared to them, he'd never have anything of consequence to offer someone like her.

To his infinite relief, Mrs. Lindstrom called over Courtney and what's her name. The wedding coordinator positioned the bridesmaids to the left of the altar and the groomsmen to the right. The reverend took his place front and center.

Sam took a seat midway down the aisle. Several of the groomsmen practiced seating Becker's parents and grandparents.

"Mom, you sit there." Paige motioned toward the first pew. "Dad? Lila?" She fluttered her hand toward the foyer. "Per tradition, my maid of honor is going to walk down the aisle and stand in my place tonight."

Wait. What?

He hadn't attended many weddings—okay, none—but if Lila walked down the aisle on the arm of Paige's father, did that mean she'd also be saying vows to Paige's groom?

Scowling, he went rigid.

Tristan's eyes narrowed an instant before widening. "Paige, darling?"

Paige was already halfway down the aisle following after her father and Lila. The three of them turned toward Tristan.

Becker rubbed his chin. "I was thinking…"

Of all the selfish… He fumed. Were these people completely insensitive or just totally clueless? Outraged on behalf of Lila's feelings, Sam clenched and unclenched his fists. Or was his fury really more about his?

Tristan started up the aisle. "If there is going to be a proxy bride, there ought to be a proxy groom, too. Don't you agree, sweetheart?"

Paige and Tristan exchanged a quick, significant glance.

Her face lit up. "You're right. How brilliant of you to think of it."

Tristan stopped beside Sam. "I realize we don't know each other very well…"

Sam's eyes darted left and then right. Was Becker talking to him?

"…but tonight would you stand in my place?"

What was Becker playing at here?

"Instead of me, Sam." Tristan's eyes appeared owlish behind his glasses. "I think you'd be perfect to go through the motions with Lila." His cheeks lifted. "What do you say?"

Was Becker actually trying to be nice to him? Be his friend?

At a sudden loss for words, Sam's gaze zeroed in like a pigeon coming home to roost on Lila. She appeared as surprised by Tristan's offer as he.

"W-would it be okay with you, Lila?" He swallowed. "Unless you'd rather…"

An emotion he couldn't read flickered in her eyes. "I'd—" She moistened her bottom lip.

He stopped breathing.

"I'd like that," she whispered.

"Excellent." Smiling, Paige hustled her father and Lila toward the back of the church.

"I think you and I got off on the wrong foot." Tristan cocked his head. "A false start. Isn't that what you call it in football? I don't know a lot about football."

Not a surprise to Sam.

"But I do know you make her happy."

"She makes me happy," he rasped.

He found himself mildly shocked to find it true. When had that happened? When had Lila Penry become essential to his world?

Becker extended his hand. And Sam decided to forgive the guy—goofy as he was—for being Lila's former boyfriend.

He shook Tristan's hand. Because what mat-

tered was now, right? And right now he wanted...
What did he want?

Tabling that to ponder later, he took Tristan's
designated position at the altar. The real groom
joined his real bride on the front row to oversee
the practice session. The wedding coordinator
cued the organist.

Lila appeared on Mr. Lindstrom's arm. In her
hands she held a paper plate decorated with gift
bows and trailing ribbon. A proxy bouquet? Was
that a thing?

Then his gaze locked with hers. And he forgot
to think about anything or anyone else. She was
so beautiful. A dream. His dream?

All those years, how did he never see it? How
achingly lovely she was. How had he missed it?

One day, she was going to make some man a
glorious bride. A wonderful wife.

Some man?

Like a regal queen, she floated toward him.
Nothing but her mattered. The music swelled.
His heart thundered.

At last, she and Paige's father stood beside
him. He turned to face the reverend. The music
ceased. The minster said something. But his
surroundings had faded. The edges of reality
blurred.

In response to the reverend's question, Mr.
Lindstrom took Lila's hand and placed it in

Sam's. A faint smile on his distinguished features, Paige's father gave Lila a quick peck on the cheek before stepping away and settling into the pew beside his wife.

More words from the minister. With occasional interruptions by the wedding coordinator to clarify certain details for Paige and Tristan.

Lila's hand felt cold in his. Was she okay? He turned toward her. With her attention still on the reverend, he could tell nothing from her expression. She pulled away slightly, and his heart jackhammered.

Was she wishing he was Tristan? Had she been sorry when Tristan made Sam his stand-in?

But she only handed the paper-bow bouquet to Paige's cousin. Then she faced him. How was she standing there so calm and collected?

Sam was drowning, but she'd always been braver than him. Refusing to be less than true to herself in high school. No matter the ridicule from other girls like Courtney.

His eyes found hers again. And her eyes rocked him. Forcing him to declare a truth his heart was only just beginning to acknowledge. Like a lifeline, he grasped hold of both her hands.

The reverend droned on, speaking words not meant for him and Lila. *Not yet*... His heart sped up a little.

Cameras clicked, and flashes went off behind them. Fireworks? Or was he seeing stars?

She gave him an uncertain smile. "Sam," she whispered.

Helping him find his breath. Grounding him. "Lila."

Grateful, he twined his fingers through hers. And held on for dear life. A life with her? Was that possible for someone like him?

When she let go of his hand, he jolted.

She nudged her chin at the groomsman on his right. "Pretend to take the ring."

Oh. Right. Yeah. That.

Expecting nothing but air, he was surprised when the groomsman deposited something into his palm. Like a rookie, he fumbled. There was a collective gasp, as if this was the real deal.

His Adam's apple bobbed. Maybe…maybe it was. But although he'd never been a receiver, he managed to recover the object in the nick of time.

Lila's lips quirked. He relaxed a notch. She held out her left hand.

He slipped the tiny green rubber band on her third finger. Lifting her hand, he brushed his lips across her fingers.

She shivered slightly and gave him the smallest of glances out of the corner of her eye, but it warmed him. And sent his heart clanging in his ears.

When it was his turn to receive a ring, she proved less clumsy than he. Of course, for him, the "ring" was nothing but air.

Lots more talk. None of which registered with him. Until the minister told him he could kiss his "bride."

He dropped his hand to her waist, pulling her closer. Her gray-blue eyes jerked to his. Did she want him to kiss her? He held back, trying to read her features. And lived an agonizing eternity in that split second.

But with a small nod, her lips parted, and she lifted her face. His heart flooded with a strange joy unlike any he'd known before. She closed her eyes, and he brushed his mouth over hers. She tasted exactly as he'd imagined.

Peppermint.

At first, her lips were tentative. But then she moved her hands to his shoulders. And she leaned into him. On the toes of her boots, she staked her claim on more of his mouth.

She'd already laid claim to his heart.

At the same instant, they both became aware of the cheers and clapping that had broken out in the chapel. They sprang apart. She ducked her head, a blush staining her cheeks.

Mr. and Mrs. Lindstrom were on their feet. So were Paige and Tristan. Even the wedding coordinator was grinning. Sam didn't let go of Lila's hand.

"By the power vested in me by the state of North Carolina, I now pronounce this man and woman…"

In his head, he understood this wasn't real. It wasn't their names the minister was speaking. But it felt real. More real than anything that had ever happened to him.

When Lila smiled at him, the surge of feeling blindsided him. Her hand clasped in his, to the bridal party's delight, he lifted their arms in a victory salute. She laughed. Was she feeling even a tenth of what he was feeling?

The organ pealed out a chord. And they were walking—no, running—down the aisle for the foyer. The coordinator began sending the first pair of attendants out after them.

They only had a moment. But it was enough. Enough for one more quick kiss.

"Not too fast. Not too slow," the coordinator admonished.

"Just right." His lips grazed her forehead.

And it was.

Chapter Eight

After the rehearsal, on the cobblestone terrace behind the inn, Lila waited for Sam to return with their plates of food.

Snow covered the vale around the resort, but gas heaters emitted enough warmth for the bridal party to enjoy a rehearsal dinner underneath the stars.

Blue twinkle lights strung around the perimeter of the terrace provided a touch of winter wonderland. Festooned with multicolored strands of light, a woodland Christmas tree lent a festive feel to the outdoor space. From the large riverstone fireplace, servers doled out slices of pizza.

Weaving his way between the clusters of linen-draped round tables, Sam returned with their food.

"Butternut squash and sage pizza for you." He sank into the cushioned seat next to her. "Pepperoni pizza for me. I'm a man of simple tastes."

Lila made sure he saw her roll her eyes. He laughed. The flickering flame from the thick ivory candle in the lantern globe cast a glow over his ruddy, handsome features.

"So this is how the other half lives? Wood-fired pizza." He smirked. "With seasonally inspired flavors."

"Hush." She nudged him with her shoulder. "Stop making fun and eat your pizza."

Sam grinned at her before taking a large bite.

Later, the bridal party gathered closer to the fireplace to enjoy hot cocoa and s'mores, fresh off the fire. Somehow, he snagged one of the love seats grouped by the fire.

The hum of conversation around Lila and Sam provided a cozy buffer. Insulating them from the rest of the group. Making it feel as if they were alone with each other in front of the roaring fire.

He tucked the red tartan blanket around her shoulders. "Want anything else to eat?"

"No, thank you."

She shook her head. Full of wonder that somehow she—klutzy, frizzy-haired Lila Penry—had managed to find herself in this unbelievable fairy-tale setting with Sam Gibson. She wanted to pinch herself to make sure she wasn't dreaming.

But on second thought, if she was dreaming, she never wanted to wake up.

As people mixed and mingled around the terrace, his face wore a bemused look. "Emma Cate would love it here. She'd think she was a princess."

"She is a princess."

Not unlike how Lila felt right now.

Sam smiled.

However, like flies in her happily-ever-after ointment, Courtney and Madison hovered off to the side, whispering. The bridal couple drifted by.

Lila tilted her head. "Princess Paige has certainly found her Prince Charming."

The smile faded from Sam's eyes. His expression tightened. "So where does that leave you?"

She wasn't sure how to respond. She wasn't about to admit that Sam had figured largely in her own girlhood fantasies of Prince Charming.

Instead, she said the first thing that came to her mind. "Are you cold?" She extended one end of the blanket. "We can share."

He cocked his head. "Are you flirting with me, Lila Penry?"

"Uh... I—I—" Her face flushed.

"Because in certain societies—" a corner of his mouth quirked "—offering to share a blanket is tantamount to a marriage proposal."

Her mouth opened and closed like a fish on a hook.

"Now that you mention it, though, I am feeling

slightly cold." Patting the space between them, he gave her a lopsided smile. "Maybe you should scoot closer."

A glint in his eyes, he draped his arm across the back of the seat. She slid over underneath his arm.

"Feels warmer already." He rested his cheek on the top of her cap. "I could get used to this."

So could she.

He held her against his side. She could feel the rise and fall of his chest. The sound of his steady breathing.

"Are you okay with this?" His voice contained a note of uncertainty.

She was better than okay with this. But she sensed he meant more than just their close proximity.

"Yes," she said, unable to trust herself to say anything more.

Snuggled together, they sat underneath the indigo velvet sky. Pinpoints of light twinkled overhead.

Keeping his voice low, he pointed out constellations he knew. But it was his face she watched, not the stars.

Standing at the altar with Sam had felt surreal. The culmination of every girlhood fantasy, only better. Because he was so much more than the handsome football jock she'd idolized from afar.

In the last three weeks, he'd shed the aloofness he'd worn like a shield throughout high school. A barricade that kept everyone at arm's length. For some reason, though, he'd let her in.

Opening his heart. Sharing his fears for Emma Cate and his insecurities about his father. She recognized he'd given her a rare gift. The gift of himself.

Giving her tantalizing, intriguing glimpses of the real Sam Gibson. A good, trustworthy man. Emma Cate's beloved daddy.

And when he looked at her the way he was looking at her now—she could almost believe he was truly hers. At least, for this one impossibly wonderful wedding weekend.

On the bedside table, her cell buzzed.

Lila opened one eye. Sunlight leaked from behind the curtain panels. *Happy is the bride the sun shines upon.*

The cell buzzed again.

She reached for the phone. When she saw the caller, she couldn't help but smile. "H-hello?"

"Rise and shine, sleepyhead."

She pursed her lips. "Why do you presume I've not been up and at 'em for hours? Getting in a morning run around the property? Working out in the gym?"

"Have you been doing any of those things?"

She rolled her tongue in her cheek. "No."

"Didn't think so." Sam chuckled. "I know you, remember?"

It did seem as if they'd known one another forever.

"Are you still wearing your Christmas cat pj's?"

She could feel the splotches of color staining her cheeks. Despite the pains she'd taken with her wardrobe recently, he would remember that first morning. With her hair in a pineapple. The crazy cat lady look.

"No, Mr. Paint Contractor." She pursed her lips. "I'm wearing my Christmas penguin pj's today."

He laughed.

"Anyway...did you catch Emma Cate on the phone last night?"

It had been after ten o'clock when the s'mores party broke up. She'd been afraid Emma Cate would already be asleep at her grandparents'.

"I did." His voice rasped pleasurably, causing goose bumps to form on her arms. "She and her grandma were watching reruns of *The Andy Griffith Show.*"

Lila flopped backward onto the pillow. "I love that show."

"Me, too."

She heard the smile in his voice.

"Anyway, I just wanted to make sure you were

awake before I headed out to snowshoe the trails around the inn with the guys."

"Brrrr..." Shivering in sympathy, she burrowed deeper under the duvet. "Better you than me."

"And... I just wanted to hear your voice."

For the love of Monet. Be still, my heart.

She hugged the cell against her cheek. "I—I can't wait to see you at the chapel later."

"Me, too." After a beat of silence, he cleared his throat. "So what's on the bridesmaid agenda this morning?"

Phone clutched to her ear, she stared at the ceiling overhead. "Wedding day pampering prep—nails, hair and makeup."

"Ugh..." he teased. "Better you than me."

Her lips twitched. "Who knew Sam Gibson was such a comedian?"

"I'm full of surprises."

Yes, he was. Hidden depths, too.

"I should go...the guys are about ready to head out." Yet he didn't hang up. "I'll find you later, and we can walk over together, okay?"

She smiled. "Okay."

"You're not going to go back to sleep when I hang up, are you, lazybones?"

Hardly. As usual, the mere sound of his voice was enough to set dragonflies to doing somersaults in her belly.

"I'm awake. Wide-awake now."

Sam Gibson was better than any alarm clock she'd ever met.

"Are your cute toes touching the floor?"

He thought her toes were cute!

She flung aside the covers. Sitting upright, she swung her legs over the side of the bed. "Yes, they are."

"You just sat up, didn't you?"

She laughed. "Goodbye, Sam. I'm hanging up now."

He said farewell, and this time he did get off the phone.

She got in the shower, going through her hair-care routine. Finishing, she slipped into the pink silk kimono Paige had given her bridesmaids to wear while they were getting ready for the wedding.

Coming out of the bathroom, she found a tray on the desk, containing a carafe of coffee and a steaming, freshly baked cinnamon roll. There was also a note, written in Paige's elegant scrawl.

Thought you might sleep in and miss breakfast. Here's something to tide you over till lunch.

After eating her fill, she left the tray outside her room on the carpet and padded two doors down the hallway to the bridal suite. When she arrived, the salon providers were still setting up for the pre-ceremony pampering.

Paige immediately left her mother and came over to hug Lila.

"Today is your big day."

Paige quivered with excitement. "I can't believe it's finally here."

"Ladies, if each of you would be so kind as to claim one of the salon chairs." Mrs. Lindstrom opened her palms. "Let the pampering commence."

Christmas carols played softly from the speakers.

In their matching cherry blossom robes, Lila and the others rotated between the mani-pedi station and several makeup chairs. Each would take a longer turn at the hairstyling base of operations.

Leaning her head against the cushion of the mani-pedi chair, Lila closed her eyes, riding the wave of relaxation. Letting her thoughts drift.

Today might be Paige's big day. But yesterday had been perhaps the best day of her life.

She smiled a secret smile, meant only for herself. No perhaps about it. Yesterday *had* been the best day of her life.

When servers arrived with popovers and warm white mushroom soup, Paige handed out tokens of gratitude—beautiful pearl earrings—to her bridesmaids.

And Lila, being Lila, accidentally knocked over her glass of water.

Dabbing at the stain spreading across the lap of her kimono with her napkin, she left the group in search of a hand towel. She was getting ready to enter the suite bathroom when she heard voices on the other side of the partially open door.

Not wanting to eavesdrop on a private conversation, she was about to return to the living room when she caught her name.

"—Lila Penry! With Sam Gibson."

A searing heat licked at her neck.

"What does someone like him see in her?"

She told herself to walk away, but she couldn't seem to get her feet to move.

"Calamity Lila hasn't changed a bit." Courtney gave a throaty laugh. "And I don't mean that in a positive way."

Her mouth trembled.

The truth hurts, Frizzy Hair.

And she made a startling realization. The mean-girl voice in her head sounded an awful lot like Courtney Askew. Once upon an elementary school nightmare, hadn't she and Courtney been in the same second-grade class?

She might not have changed, but she'd given Courtney and Madison too much credit. They hadn't changed, either.

"You know Sam and I…" Courtney purred. "At one time, he was so into me, but with that father of his, eventually I had to end it with him."

"Wise move," Madison said in her screechy, nasal voice. "Look where he ended up. Still in Truelove. And a house painter, of all things."

Courtney giggled.

Lila fisted her hands. Sam was a commercial and residential paint contractor. A respected, successful business owner, she wanted to shout.

It was one thing for them to trash her, but she'd paint dogs playing poker on crushed velvet before she'd let them belittle Sam. They were the same gossipy snobs they'd always been. Lila stepped toward the door, ready to confront them.

"She probably had to pay him to get him to take her to Paige's wedding," Madison crowed.

Cheeks burning, she unclenched her hands and stepped away. In a sense, she had paid him to take her to the wedding. Emma Cate's art lessons in exchange for Sam being her plus-one.

Was that how he saw their little deal? She winced. Simply a business transaction?

"And that crazy hair of hers! Seriously."

One of them moved toward the door. Unwilling to face further ridicule, she beat a hasty retreat.

Had she embarrassed Sam yesterday? He'd seemed to be enjoying himself. He liked to tease and flirt with her. Perhaps she'd imagined something more between them. Wishful thinking?

Maybe Courtney and Madison were right. What did she know about boyfriends? She'd only had one—Tristan. And look how that had turned out. She couldn't even hang on to him.

And Lila made up her mind, she would embarrass Sam no further. Enough with the crazy hair. If she couldn't beat them, she might as well join them.

Stalking over to the hairstyling station, she flopped into the empty chair. "Would it be possible to straighten my hair today?"

The stylist, a middle-aged woman with a short cap of—*yep*—straight brown hair, frowned. "You mean with a flat iron?"

Lila nodded at the woman's reflection in the mirror. "Exactly."

Standing behind the chair, the stylist ran practiced fingers through her tresses. "But you have such pretty hair, honey."

"It's not the hair I want."

More importantly, apparently not the sort of hair Sam liked.

"If you're sure…"

She made a face at the mirror. "I'm sure."

Two hours later, she barely recognized herself in the mirror. Turning this way and that, she admired her new look from every angle.

It was different. Very…flat. And straight. Not at all like her usual cloud of hair.

She lifted her chin. But elegant like Paige. Chic. Sleek perfection.

Take that, mean second-grade Courtney. No more crazy, frizzy hair now.

The makeup artist was her final stop. Afterward, Paige asked her to come into her bedroom to help her slip into her bridal gown. So totally gorgeous. So totally Paige.

"You're going to knock Tristan's glasses right off his face."

Paige and her mother laughed.

"You think so?"

Lila nodded. "I know so."

Her mother fastened the pearl choker around Paige's slim neck. Lila draped the white faux fur stole over her bare shoulders. Not what she would've chosen for such a snowy winter venue, but to each her own.

The three of them admired the final result in the floor-length mirror. Paige's gaze flitted to Lila. "You're still in your kimono. I've kept you longer than I should."

"I'm your maid of honor."

"The best maid of honor ever, but Mom will take me down to the sleigh." She shooed Lila to the door. "You need to get into your dress."

Back in her own room, it didn't take long to

change into the long green velvet dress Paige had chosen for the bridesmaids to wear.

Sam texted her that he'd be there in five minutes, giving her plenty of time for a last bit of preening in front of the bathroom mirror.

Dangly pearl earrings? *Check.*

She adjusted the green satin bow around her waist and brushed her fingertips across the rich sheen of the velvet.

Makeup unsmeared? *Check.*

Hairdo magnificent and intact? *Che—*

At the knock, she turned her head. "Coming."

Gathering her wrap, she hurried over, imagining his surprise at the new Lila Penry.

Flinging the door open, she stepped into the hallway. The door creaked shut behind her. She drank in the sight of him.

Wow, he cleans up good.

In a charcoal suit coat and pants, he didn't look up as he fiddled with the ends of a scarlet silk tie. "I'm hoping you know what to do with this?"

"No problem." She took the ends from him. "Cross. Under and over. Pull through the center. Loop through the knot. And tighten." She patted the tie. "Voilà."

It was only then he appeared to get his first good look at the new Lila Penry. "What happened to your hair?"

Forgetting she'd been indoors all day, she

touched the top of her recently tamed curls. Had a bird pooped on her head?

That had happened to her once.

His eyes narrowed, still fixed on her hair. "What did you do?"

She smiled. "I straightened it."

"You what?" He stared at her as if in horror. A pulse thrummed in his handsome jaw. "Why?"

"Because…" Were some things not self-evident? "Because…"

He took hold of her arm. "How long will it take you to unstraighten it?"

She gaped at him.

"You-you can fix it, right?" His blue eyes widened. "You can put it back like it was?" He gestured in the general direction of her hair. "Please tell me this isn't permanent."

Chin quivering, she bit her lip. "I thought it looked sophisticated. Polished."

"It's not the real you." He pushed her toward the door. "How long? You're due at the chapel in thirty minutes for pre-wedding photos with Paige."

The real her? He wanted the real her—the ungainly, walking disaster her? Was he out of his mind?

She'd done everything in her power—spent an enormous amount of money on hair products—

just so she wouldn't embarrass the gorgeous Sam Gibson with the real her.

"I liked your hair the way it was, Lila."

Rendered speechless and immobile, she couldn't have been more shocked if he'd told her he preferred beef barbecue over pork.

Placing his hands on her shoulders, he turned her toward the door. Taking the key card clutched in her hand, he swiped it and pushed the door open.

He touched the small of her back. "Lila."

And she snapped into action. "Fifteen minutes."

"I'll wait out here."

She hurried inside. The door swung shut behind her.

Fifteen minutes to wet her hair. She rushed into the bathroom. Fifteen minutes to wreck the gloriously smooth, shiny, light-refracting silk the stylist had spent hours creating.

Careful not to ruin her dress or her makeup, she used a spray bottle to douse her locks. It wasn't long before her unruly curls reverted to their usual riotous disorder. She finger-combed her tresses into a semblance of respectability.

Fighting tears, she swept a hank of hair from both sides of her face and fastened it at the crown of her head with the pearl clip Paige had given the bridesmaids at her bridal shower. The rest of her hair cascaded in soft waves across her shoulders and down her back.

Then an altogether revolutionary idea flitted across her consciousness. Sam said he liked her hair the way it *was*. She nearly reeled. Which meant...

Sam *liked* her hair. Sam liked *her* hair. Sam liked her *hair*.

Lila put her hand over her rapidly pounding heart.

Either he had extremely bad taste in hair or... Or... She put her fingers to her lips.

Don't be ridiculous. That wasn't a thought worth finishing. Completely out of the realm of possibility.

Wasn't it?

Chapter Nine

When Lila reemerged from her room, Sam's first reaction was relief to see her hair restored to its original splendor.

She was quiet on the way to the chapel, but he didn't think too much about it. He hung back, letting the photographer do his thing with the pre-wedding pictures.

Lila smiled for the photos in all the right moments, but there was a pensive quality about her. Like she had something on her mind.

During a lull when the photographer snapped photos of the Lindstroms, Sam headed over to her. "What's the matter?"

Her shoulders hunched. "I'm so klutzy."

"I've never seen you do anything remotely clumsy."

She chewed her bottom lip. "Only because you're a good influence on me."

He liked the notion of someone believing him a good influence.

"Suppose I trip over my feet or my dress?" She gestured. "Suppose I drop the ring? Suppose—"

"Relax." He cupped her elbow in the palm of his hand. "I'm the one who almost dropped the ring. Not you. You've got this."

She straightened. "You think so?"

"I know so."

Wedding guests trickled into the chapel. Lila, the rest of the bridesmaids and Paige disappeared.

He decided to sit on the groom's side—a better angle from which to gaze at Lila during the ceremony. The minister stood at the altar. Tristan and the groomsmen positioned themselves at the front. The music changed.

One by one the bridesmaids made the trip to the front of the church. *Ho-hum. Yawn city.*

Then, clutching her bouquet, Lila took her walk down the aisle. And his heart slammed against his ribs.

Looking neither left nor right, her gray-blue eyes remained focused on her destination. A small furrow creased the space between her brows. When she made it to her designated spot, her gaze flitted over the assembled guests until finding him.

His heart lifting, he gave her an unobtrusive thumbs-up. And her shoulders loosened a notch.

Taking her duties very seriously, the flower girl meticulously distributed the flower petals down the center of the aisle, earning smiles from the guests.

He sniffed. Paige's niece was cute, but at his wedding he was sure Emma Cate would make an even cuter flower girl.

Whoa. His wedding? His gaze cut to Lila. Where had that come from? But he had a sneaking suspicion he knew from what source the idea had suddenly taken root.

The bride came next. Mr. Lindstrom did the handoff of the bride to Tristan. But Sam only had eyes for Lila. In his humble but accurate opinion, she far outshone the rest of the bridesmaids. Paige, too.

Lila was funny. And smart. And kind.

Not to mention gorgeous in that dress. A pit in his stomach knotted at thought of her hair. His fingers itched to know the softness of the curls cascading down her back. She was beautiful.

And he mentally kicked himself for not telling her so.

Why had he not told her she was beautiful? Because he was an inarticulate idiot. *Way to prove the stupid jock stereotype, Gibson.*

The rest of the ceremony went off without a

hitch. After she successfully negotiated the bouquet pass, he figured she breathed a sigh of relief. But he slowly became aware of the conflicted expression in her eyes. And where her gaze had fixed.

On the bridal couple.

He tried telling himself that was part of the whole maid-of-honor deal. She was concentrating. Not wanting to miss her cue.

Or—his gut lurched—maybe it wasn't the bridal couple she was looking at. Only Tristan. Sam stiffened.

Suppose she did still have feelings for him? The notion of Lila still being in love with Tristan—with anybody—made his stomach roil.

Why did it matter? What was it to him? He was nothing more than just her plus-one. She'd been clear from the beginning about the terms of this wedding weekend.

It shouldn't matter if she was in love with Tristan Becker or not. Not his concern. He had his own struggles. His business. Emma Cate. Enough for any man.

But he did care. They were…friends. And if he were in her position, watching someone he loved marry someone else…

If he were watching Lila marry someone else—

His heart thudded with an almost physical

pain. She'd put on a brave face this weekend. But now, confronted with reality, she must be feeling devastated.

And he remembered what she'd said to him when they were driving to the resort that first day. Asking him to make sure she didn't humiliate herself.

He hadn't thought much about it at the time. Chalked it up to nerves about the whole clumsy phobia she believed about herself.

But suppose it was something more? So much more if anyone in Truelove or the wedding party—or Paige—ever found out her true feelings for Tristan? And that was the one thing he couldn't bear—to see her pain on display for the world.

Setting aside his own mixed-up feelings, he had to be there for her. Get her through Paige's wedding day.

Champing at the bit, he became desperate for the ceremony to end. Desperate to reach Lila. To comfort her. To help her pick up the shattered pieces of her heart.

The recessional seemed to go slow-mo. The flower girl was the first to head after the bridal couple. Escorted by Tristan's best friend, the doctor, Lila was next to head back up the aisle. And row by agonizing row, the groomsmen ushered out the guests.

"Excuse me." Sam muscled his way through the crowd clustered outside on the steps of the chapel. "Excuse me."

Searching for Lila, he scanned the crowd. Laughing, chatting, the solemn moments over, bridesmaids and groomsmen appeared eager for the party to commence. Guests began making their way through the trees toward the reception hall.

The hotel had arranged for flower-bedecked sleighs to transport the wedding party. Paige, Tristan and their parents were whisked away first.

Where was—

Finally spotting her, he fast walked in her direction.

"Sam, I—"

He enfolded her in his arms. "You did great, baby." He kissed her hair. *Wow, she smells good.* "So great."

She laid her cheek against his chest. His heartbeat accelerated at her nearness. She sighed.

"Thank you for being here with me." Her voice wobbled. "I—I don't know how I would have gotten through this weekend without you."

Closing his eyes, he rested his chin on her head. "It's going to be okay. Maybe it doesn't feel that way right now, but someday this weekend will seem like a bad dream that never happened."

Her head snapped up, nearly clipping his jaw. "A bad dream?" She took an abrupt step away from him.

"Ma'am? Sir?" The driver of one of the sleighs beckoned. "It's your turn."

Lila allowed the liveried driver to hand her into the carriage. When Sam climbed in after her, she gave him an unreadable look.

Clicking his tongue under his teeth, the driver snapped the reins, and with a jolting lurch, the horse moved forward, setting the carriage in motion.

Lowering her gaze, she made a great show of tucking her skirts around her. His heart raced. He did not—he absolutely did not—like not being able to see her face. She wore her heart and her every emotion on her features.

His fears ratcheted. Or was that exactly why she wouldn't look at him? She didn't want him to see… She didn't want him to guess her true feelings for Tristan.

Trotting around the glade of trees, the chestnut-colored horse tossed its mane and whinnied as the carriage glided over the snow.

"Please, please look at me, Lila." Taking her chin into his hand, he drew her gaze upward to his. "We'll get through the rest of this day together. I promise I won't leave you, not for a minute."

Her eyes locked onto his.

"It guts me to see you hurting like this." His palm cupped the side of her face. Seemingly of its own volition, his thumb traced the apple of her cheek. "But I'll never breathe a word of this to anyone."

A tremulous look filled her eyes.

"I know you don't feel about me the way you feel about Tristan—"

She jerked. "Tristan? What are you talking about?"

Was she really going to make him say it?

He clenched his jaw so hard his teeth ached. "You're still in love with Tristan, but it doesn't—"

"I'm not in love with Tristan."

His thumb stopped moving. "Wait. I… I…"

"Is that what you were talking about before we got in the sleigh?"

"Well, yeah." Dropping his hand, he straightened. "What did you think I was talking about?"

She gave him a slow smile. "It doesn't matter." She fluttered her hand. "Where in the world did you get the idea I was in love with Tristan?"

"When you… The day we… You said…" He sagged against the red leather upholstery. "So for the record, you're telling me you are not in love with Tristan Becker?"

She raised her palm. "I am not, nor I have ever been, in love with Tristan Becker."

He blinked at her. How had he so completely jumped to the wrong conclusion? Unless the thought of losing her...*losing her friendship*... had made him overly sensitive. And delusional.

"That's..." He swallowed hard. "That's good news. Great news." The best news.

Welcoming lights from the inn loomed ahead on the path.

She gave him a funny smile. "I'm glad you're pleased."

"I can think of something that would please me more."

Leaning forward, he captured both sides of her face between his palms. He held her gently, giving her the option to pull away. But she didn't.

She closed her eyes. Her lips parted. And taking that as a yes, he kissed her. It wasn't as sweet a kiss as the kiss at the rehearsal last night. But he'd been waiting for this chance all day.

And she was kissing him back. Tentative, her fingertips touched the stubble on his chin. The fragrance of her shampoo enveloped him. Intoxicating his senses with her essence.

This kiss held an intensity that hadn't been there before. A wholeness. A rightness that stole his breath.

Locked in each other's arms, at first he didn't realize the sleigh had come to a standstill. A camera flashed. The driver cleared his throat.

With great reluctance Sam pulled his mouth from hers.

The sleigh had stopped at the entrance of the inn. They'd attracted a sizable crowd. There were a few discreet handclaps.

She blushed. A small vein pulsed in the hollow of her throat. And he was pleased his kiss had that effect on her.

"Perhaps I should've tipped the driver to take the longer route." He touched his finger to her dangling earring, setting it in motion. "The 'over the river, through the wood, on the other side of the county and around again' route."

Lila smiled.

Stepping out, he offered her his hand. And they made their way into the banquet hall.

Paige had outdone herself in putting together the wedding reception. Great food. Great fun. And he enjoyed dancing the slow dances with Lila.

Now that he knew she wasn't pining for the groom, he magnanimously decided not to dislike Becker. Or at least, not as intensely.

If it hadn't been for missing Emma Cate, he would've wanted nothing more than to stay here with Lila in his arms forever.

On Sunday, he and Lila attended the farewell lunch. Everyone said their goodbyes to Paige and

Tristan. Standing on the steps outside the hotel, they watched the newlyweds drive off, cans clanging, until the car disappeared from view.

"I don't know when I'll see Paige again," Lila said, her voice wistful. "After the honeymoon, they'll be moving to Boston for Tristan's new job."

Boston? So very far away from Truelove. *Nice.*

She raised her eyebrow. "Why are you smiling?"

His mouth quirked. "No reason."

At the front desk, they checked out of the resort. Duffel bag on his shoulder, he was wheeling her suitcase across the lobby toward the exit when Mrs. Lindstrom stopped them.

Paige's mother threw her arms around Lila. "I am so thrilled for you."

What? He mouthed to Lila.

Clasped in Mrs. Lindstrom's embrace, she shook her head.

Releasing her, Mrs. Lindstrom took one of his hands and one of Lila's in hers. "I wish you both the merriest of Christmases." Her eyes shone. "Please tell your mom and dad, Lila, how pleased I am."

"Okay…" Her eyes cut to him and back to Paige's mother. "Sure."

At the truck, he tucked their bags behind the cab. "What was that about?"

She shrugged. "No clue." She gazed one last time around the resort property. "I never imagined it would turn out to be such a wonderful weekend."

Him, too.

Sam helped her into the truck. Slipping behind the wheel, he started the ignition.

Lila sighed. "Back to reality."

He spared one lingering glance at the inn in the rearview mirror. Lying on the seat between them, her cell buzzed inside her purse.

Without examining the screen, she took out the cell and silenced it, setting it aside. "I guess you're looking forward to Emma Cate coming home on Friday."

He looked at her out of the corner of his eye. "I am."

A beat of silence. Then—

"Hard to believe Christmas will be upon us in less than a month. I guess you'll be busy finishing the library job."

Sam gripped the wheel. "I guess so." He set his jaw. "You'll have classes to teach again tomorrow."

Lila pursed her lips. "I'm sure we'll both find ourselves with lots to do before Christmas."

With a sinking feeling, he realized with their wedding bargain complete and her house painted, they'd revert to their pre–painting, wedding weekend status. More acquaintances than friends.

After they crossed the mountain pass, the farther they descended, the sparser the snow on the ground became. And with every mile closer to Truelove, his spirits sank further. The future—his future—seemed unbearably empty.

Her phone vibrated again. She ignored it. "Think we'll get snow in Truelove tonight?"

She stared out the window at the passing winter-bare trees on the side of the road. The scenery was as bleak as he felt right now. The sky as overcast as his mood.

"Maybe."

Lips tightening, she tucked a strand of hair behind her ear. "And thus ends our weekend."

His heart thumped. That was just it. He wasn't sure exactly what he did want, but he knew he didn't want this to be an ending for them.

The cell buzzed. Whoever was calling her was nothing if not persistent.

He beat a nervous tap on the steering wheel with his thumbs. "Maybe you should get that?"

She crossed her arms over her sweater. "Probably spam. I'll check when I get home."

Best-case scenario, on occasion, they might run into each other in town. He might chance upon her at Emma Cate's school. But he'd have no reason to spend time with her. No excuse to call her. Unless he did something…said something…

Yet suppose she didn't feel the same way? His throat dried up. His tongue felt glued to the roof of his mouth.

He'd never been good with words. Working with his hands all his life, he was a man who preferred action. He didn't know what to say, so he said nothing.

And whereas the trip to the inn had been full of laughter, talking over each other in excitement, now they were virtually silent. The air between them was tense. Full of emotional land mines.

He was unsure of where to go from here. Unsure where she wanted to go from here. With him.

The miles continued to tick down. Nearly home. Running out of time. Her phone had fallen silent. Like him.

He'd never been any good at relationships with women. He had a business to run. A daughter to raise. With too little energy in his life for anything else. Which was fine with him. More than fine.

Or at least, it had been. Until Lila came into his life.

It was late afternoon when he drove past the signpost on the outskirts of town. Truelove—

Where True Love Awaits. His heart pounded. The truck rattled over the bridge.

He turned into Lila's neighborhood. She stuffed her cell into her purse. He pulled into her driveway and stopped the truck. The engine idled.

She gave him a searing look. But he couldn't seem to breathe, much less speak.

Purse strap on her shoulder, she released her seat belt with a snap. He jolted. Grasping the handle, she pushed open the door and stepped out.

Sweat peppered his forehead. His chest rose and fell. His heart seized. He strangled the wheel.

Lila peered across the cab at him. "I guess this is goodb—"

"I promised my mom I'd meet her at the tree lighting in the square this evening," he said in a desperate rush of words. "Would you want to go with me?" His lungs momentarily depleted of oxygen, he inhaled sharply.

For a long, agonizing second, she just looked at him. Finally—

"Yes, I would." She smiled. "Thank you for asking."

Getting out, he put her suitcase in the house. She went upstairs to freshen up, and he texted his mom that he was in town.

His mother immediately replied. Is it true?

Brow creasing, he texted her again. Is what true? Can't wait to talk.

He quickly fired off one last text to let his mom know he'd see her and Phil on the village green in ten.

Lila came downstairs and tucked her phone into her coat pocket.

He looked up. "Ready?"

Smiling, she nodded.

While they were inside the house, darkness had fallen. As they drove toward the downtown area, it appeared the entire community had turned out for Truelove's annual Christmas tree lighting. He had to park two blocks from the square, and they walked the rest of the way.

At the corner between the police station and the Mason Jar, they ran into Deon.

"You sly dog, you." Deon gave him a playful shoulder punch. "Why didn't you say something, dude?"

Rubbing his shoulder, he cut his eyes at Lila. "Like 'ow'?"

Deon chuckled. "I'm not letting you off the hook that easy." He hugged Lila, taking her and Sam both by surprise. "Very romantic. Never knew he had it in him."

Sam frowned. "What's—"

Deon held up his palm. "Don't want to keep you. Lots more people looking for you two. Gotta run, but we'll talk tomorrow at work." And with that, he hurried off.

Lila's eyebrow arched. "What was that about?"

He shrugged.

Puffy snow clouds gathered in the early, velvety twilight of the December evening. Strands of white lights marked the perimeter of the square.

Crossing the street, they waded knee-deep into the throngs of Truelove citizens crowded around the gazebo. Inside the gazebo, a large, unlit Christmas fir waited for the mayor to flip the switch.

At the foot of the gazebo off to the side, they stopped to wait for his mom and stepfather to find them. As persistent as a mosquito in summer, Lila's phone began buzzing and buzzing.

His breath frosted in the wintry air. "Who's blowing up your phone?"

She checked. "AnnaBeth." She shook her head. "There's two…four…" She frowned. "AnnaBeth has left a half dozen messages."

"I hope nothing's wrong."

Putting the phone to her ear, she listened to her voice-mail messages.

On the periphery of his vision, he sighted the three elderly members of the Double Name Club in matching knitted scarves closing in on their location.

Wonder what they wanted?

"Uh… Sam…" A strange note in her voice. "AnnaBeth sent me a link to a bunch of photos." Frantically, she began scrolling through her feed.

As soon as his mother and stepfather joined them, Phil broke into the goofiest grin. *Weird, but whatever.*

"Oh honey." His mother threw her arms around him. He staggered. "She's everything I ever hoped for you and more."

Lila had gone stock-still.

Releasing him, his mother brushed a tear from her eye. "I am so thrilled."

"Mom?" His eyes cut from his mother to her. "Lila?"

She raised her phone. "I'm so, so sorry. I don't know how, but there's been a terrible mis—"

"About time," GeorgeAnne Allen harrumphed.

"So wonderful," Miss ErmaJean cooed.

IdaLee gave him a look. "So unexpected."

What was going on?

Rushing over, Myra Penry engulfed her daughter in a hug. "Oh sweetheart, Dad and I are so pleased."

Lila looked like she wanted to cry.

Eyes misty, Cliff Penry extended his hand. "Welcome to the family, son."

Mouth gaping, Sam automatically grasped her father's hand.

Sudden light blazed from the fir inside the gazebo. Mr. Penry let go of his hand. Everyone angled toward the structure.

Gasps of delight echoed around the green. Atop the tree, a star burned brightly, pushing away the inky blackness of the night.

"Lila?" he hissed in her ear. "What is going on?"

"Everyone thinks…" She bit her lip. "Oh, Sam."

"Everyone thinks what?" he grunted.

"That we're…" She gulped. "Engaged."

Chapter Ten

Standing beside their friends and family beneath the shining lights of the Christmas tree in the gazebo, he looked as stunned as Lila felt.

If it weren't so tragically messed up, it would have been comical.

But she felt far from laughing. It was all she could do to refrain from bursting into tears. She'd save those for the privacy of her bedroom.

She put her hand to her throat, the heat of her skin warming through her glove to her palm. Her face and neck were probably the color of a tomato. Embarrassment didn't begin to cover the myriad of emotions racing through her mind.

Did calamity follow her every step, just waiting to pounce? Did humiliation lurk around every bend? How had this happened? A cruel prank? A genuine mistake?

Whichever, it was too much, too soon. And ef-

fectively ended any chance of something growing between them before it had scarcely begun.

Her head throbbed. The ramifications of this
latest catastrophe sizzled her brain. Sam Gibson
would set a new Truelove High record for fast-
est time down the field—*the block*—to distance
himself from her. Who could blame him?

She was a walking, breathing disaster waiting to happen. And this time, he'd been caught
in the aftershock.

Oh no. Stricken, she gaped at him. Maybe he
thought she'd done this on purpose. Set him up.
Deliberately entrapped him.

Even if she didn't get the artist-in-residence
position, after this there was no way she could
stay in Truelove. She was too utterly disgraced.
But somehow she had to save the situation for
him.

Perhaps a little comic relief wasn't such a bad
idea, after all.

She screwed her face into a semblance of a
smile. "Reports of our engagement have been
greatly—"

"If y'all would give Lila and me a minute." He
tugged at her arm. "We'll be right back."

"Those marvelous courtship days." Her mother
threw her father a fond look. "Lovebirds need
their privacy." The others chuckled.

A surge of volcanic warmth threatened to fry her cheeks. *Dear Lord, please...take me now.*

His mouth set in a thin straight line, Sam hauled her away. "Excuse us, please." Gripping her hand, he shouldered his way through the crowd. "Coming through."

Sam towed her toward the statue of Truelove's town founder at the edge of the green along Main. Putting the granite statue between them and any gawkers, he whipped around. "How did this happen?"

She choked back the half sob rising in her throat.

His features gentled. "Breathe." Taking her face between his callused palms, he looked into her gaze.

But when she was drowning in the azure pool of his eyes, breathing was easier said than done.

"Why does everyone think we're engaged, Lila?"

Extracting her phone from her coat, she scrolled and then held up the screen for him to see. In the picture, she was wrapped in a blanket and leaning against Sam in front of the outdoor fireplace at the resort.

He peered at the photo. "I still don't see why someone would think—"

"Look at the caption."

"*Firelight proposal.*" He frowned. "Proposal? We were only talking."

"Someone must've overheard us and jumped to the wrong conclusion."

"I don't even remember what we were… Oh." His eyes grew large. "I did say 'marriage proposal,' but I was making a joke."

"A joke?" Her chin came up. "Because Sam Gibson proposing to Lila Penry for real is just too ridiculous to be believed?"

"That's not what I meant." He scrunched his forehead. "And why is proposing to you ridiculous?"

She threw out her hands. "Because you didn't."

"Didn't isn't the same as wouldn't."

She blinked at him.

"And on the basis of one photo, someone assumed—"

"There's another one." She scrolled to the last photo in the post. "When you kissed me in the sleigh."

His eyes glinted. "As I recall, I wasn't the only one doing the kissing."

The memory of that moment sent warmth surging through her cheeks.

She pursed her lips. "I'm sorry this has become so embarrassing for you."

"I didn't say I was sorry for kissing you." His jaw tightened. "Who posted the photos?"

Who had been close enough to them to overhear their conversation that night by the fire? Everyone had been milling around. Mr. and Mrs. Lindstrom. Paige and Tristan. Courtney and Madison had been standing close by, too. But she hadn't seen them or anyone else taking photos.

Although snuggled up against Sam, she'd been a bit preoccupied. A herd of dancing reindeer could've traipsed through the cobblestone terrace and she probably wouldn't have noticed. Such was the continuing effect of Sam on her sensibilities.

She shrugged. "I don't know who originally posted the pictures. AnnaBeth's mother sent them to her. Apparently she knows Mrs. Lindstrom."

"Mrs. Lindstrom posted the photos?"

"I'm not sure. The photos have gone viral."

He flinched. She tried not to wince at his reaction. This was awful. Simply awful.

"It doesn't matter now who posted them." He crossed his arms. "What matters is where we go from here."

Miserable, she nodded. "I'll tell everyone there's been a misunderstanding."

"Hang on." He took hold of her arm. "Let's think about this first. What if we *were* engaged?"

Sam tried not to be offended at the look on her face. Was the idea of being engaged to him that hideous?

Lila tugged on a lock of her hair. "We're not engaged."

"But what if we were?" He lifted her hand. "You're still wearing my ring."

She glanced at the rubber band on her finger. "I—I forgot to take it off."

"Because I'm so forgettable?" He scowled. "Or because I'm Jason Gibson's son?"

"Neither. Any girl in Truelove would be proud to call you her fiancé." She touched his arm.

He crossed his arms. "Except you." He couldn't think straight when she touched him.

She opened her mouth and closed it again. She swallowed. "I don't blame you for being angry with me."

Was that what she thought?

He raked his hand over his head. "I'm not angry with you. This isn't your fault."

She glanced over her shoulder. "We need to set the record straight with our families."

"I think we should hold off telling them we're not engaged."

She tilted her head. "I don't understand why we're standing here arguing instead of telling them the truth."

Why *was* he arguing against coming clean? Wounded pride? Or something else?

"I think we need to consider the benefits before we go rejecting the opportunity we've been given."

"Benefits?" She frowned. "What opportunity?"

"Look at them." He jabbed his finger at their families and the three matchmakers, gathered in a huddle at the gazebo. "Who is to say they didn't conspire to create this situation?"

"Conspire?" She shook her head. "None of them were even at the wedding."

"You and I both know their spies are everywhere."

"Paranoid much, Sam?"

He jabbed his finger. "Over the last six months, those old women have hounded me to death. Setting me up with one woman after another."

"It must be simply exhausting being you." She curled her lip. "To be the object of such female admiration."

He glared. "I'm tired of going out with women I'm not interested in."

She glowered. "Maybe you should try going out with women you *are* interested in, then."

"Which is exactly why I went to Paige's wedding with you."

She reared a fraction. "Oh."

"Which is why I'm proposing—" He flushed. "—suggesting we continue our engagement."

"To get the matchmakers off your back?"

"Until Emma Cate comes home. By that time,

Truelove will have moved onto other more news-worthy items."

"You want us to pretend to be engaged for a week?"

"Everyone appeared excited by the news." He stuck his hands in his pockets. "Downright happy."

"So you're saying we should give them what they want."

Put that way, it made him sound an awful lot like his father, the con artist. And there was no one on earth he wanted to be less like.

"You're right." He slumped. "I don't know what I was thinking. We need to do the right thing and tell them the truth."

Hand in hand, they returned to the gazebo.

"Mom? Phil? Mr. and Mrs. Penry. Ladies." Taking a deep breath, he scanned the circle of faces. "There's been a mistake. Lila and I are not engaged."

His mother winked at Myra Penry. "Of course you aren't, dear."

"Good one." Cliff Penry clapped Phil on the shoulder. "These two, such comedians."

He furrowed his brow. "No. Seriously. Tell them, Lila."

"A secret engagement." GeorgeAnne eyed their hands. "Got it." She winked. "We'll keep it on the down low until you've had a chance to tell your little girl."

"You don't understand." He let go of Lila's hand. "We don't want you to get the wrong idea. I want to continue to see Lila—"

"You do?" She looked at him.

He looked at her. "I do."

She smiled.

He smiled back. "But as of right now, we are not—"

"Mum's the word. Loose lips sink ships." ErmaJean made a zipping motion over her mouth. "And until the wedding invites arrive in the mail, discretion is our middle name."

Lila sighed.

Busybody was their middle name.

"We tried." she whispered. "If you can't beat 'em, join 'em? Till Saturday?"

At her sudden reversal, he could only manage two words. "Till then."

Their wedding weekend bargain had given him more than he initially bargained for. Her, too. But he didn't mind.

His new relationship status took him off the matrimonial market. And the matchmakers, at least temporarily, off his case. Yet that was the least of the reasons he wanted everyone to believe they were engaged.

She squeezed his hand. And his pulse thrummed. He gazed at her smiling face.

He was looking for an excuse to spend time with her. He was falling for Emma Cate's art teacher. Falling hard and fast.

Now he had only to work up the courage to tell her so.

The bright white, reflective glow spilling into her bedroom the next morning could only mean one thing. Snow had fallen during the night.

Pushing aside the quilted bedspread, Lila padded over to the window. Twitching aside the curtain, she gazed out over the altered landscape. Snow had transformed Truelove into a winter wonderland.

A cold, brittle sunshine beamed down from a blue sky. And she was glad to note the street had already been cleared.

Lila checked her phone for notifications about school closings. As she expected, there were none. Flatlander schools closed at the first sign of a snowflake. But mountain residents were made of hardier stuff.

So she got dressed for school. Downstairs, she grabbed a quick breakfast. Filling a coffee tumbler to go, her attention fastened on the rubber band on the third finger of her left hand.

Tristan's best man must have swiped it off

the snowman accessory table and stuck it in his pocket. Just in case. Like the doctor he was, always prepared. Even in the event of a wedding rehearsal emergency.

Smiling, she hummed a Christmas carol. The reason she hadn't taken off the rubber band wasn't because she'd forgotten.

When she backed out of the garage, her gaze landed on Aunt IdaLee's house. For the first time, she realized how quiet her aunt had been when their "news" broke last night.

Aunt IdaLee was nobody's fool. Had she somehow seen through their charade? And if so, why hadn't she said something? Her reticence felt suddenly significant.

Easing out onto the street, Lila pushed away her doubts. Who was being paranoid now?

She headed toward Main Street. Driving around the square, she glimpsed Sam's truck and the Paint by the Numbers van parked outside the library, a few blocks from the school. She parked in the school parking lot and hurried out of the cold into the school building.

But when she reached the art room, AnnaBeth was already waiting for her. "Engaged, huh?"

Lila sagged. "Once we got home to Truelove last night, everyone kind of ambushed us." She let the tote bag slid off her shoulder. "Everything just happened so fast."

AnnaBeth rolled her eyes. "Fast is going from plus-one to date to fiancé over the course of one weekend."

"We tried to tell everyone the truth."

AnnaBeth raised her brow. "Obviously not hard enough."

"No one seemed interested in the truth."

"Maybe because everyone thinks you and Sam together are a brilliant idea." AnnaBeth smirked. "Although I wouldn't be surprised if the match-makers may be a tad miffed at being blindsided."

Lila's eyes widened. *Oh no.* Aunt IdaLee had said she had someone special picked out for Sam.

Her stomach tanked. Was her aunt's unchar-acteristic reticence because they'd messed up the matchmakers' best-laid plans? Miss GeorgeAnne and Miss ErmaJean had appeared delighted, but perhaps Aunt IdaLee hadn't yet shared her plans for Sam with her matchmaking mates.

AnnaBeth folded her arms. "Whose idea was the pretend engagement anyway?"

"Sam's."

AnnaBeth's mouth quirked. "That's interest-ing."

Lila sighed. "Not really." She filled AnnaBeth in on what had transpired.

AnnaBeth nodded. "A bait and switch."

"I told Sam it was a crazy idea."

"So why the turnaround? Why did you jump on the fake engagement bandwagon?"

Lila winced. "When you say it that way, *fake* sounds so bad."

"But so accurate."

She wasn't sure why she'd reversed course. "I didn't like seeing Sam floundering. Trying to get them to understand."

AnnaBeth laughed. "And I'm sure getting the chance to spend more time with him never for one second crossed your mind?"

"Guilty as charged." She raised her palm and let it drop. "I'm ashamed to say the opportunity proved more than I could resist. But it's only till Emma Cate gets home."

"You realize, eventually, the truth that you're only friends will come out." AnnaBeth gave her a look. "If that's really what you and Sam are to each other."

Is that what she and Sam were? Just friends?

Remembering the feel of his lips pressed against hers in the sleigh, she reddened.

"But what about California, Lila?"

She grimaced. "I'm beginning to think the whole artist-in-residence thing was a long shot."

"Thinking or hoping?"

She didn't know how to answer that.

"And what about once the truth comes out? What then?"

She swallowed. "With everything else in my life so uncertain right now, I can't look beyond the next few weeks."

"Can't or won't?" AnnaBeth shook her head. "Are you sure this pretend engagement is what you truly want to do?"

"The thing is, I like him, AnnaBeth. I really like him."

She put her arm around Lila's shoulders. "I don't want your feelings to get so caught up in make-believe that you get hurt when it ends."

"I know our time together will end when Emma Cate returns. But my heart..." She bit her lip. "My heart wants to enjoy this week."

AnnaBeth headed home. And putting any niggling concerns about the future out of her mind, Lila resolved to enjoy being with Sam. For as long as she could.

She didn't like keeping secrets from her family, though. Sam hadn't, either. He planned to talk with his mom and Phil tonight.

As soon as she finished her classes that afternoon, she headed across the square to Penry and Penry, CPA.

The office was small, a family-owned business. Just her father and mother. They'd hoped one day to pass the business to her.

Yet another way she'd disappointed them. By the time she was Emma Cate's age, it must have been obvious to everyone she wasn't cut out for accounting.

Taking a deep breath, she yanked open the glass-fronted door.

Her mom rose from behind her desk. "Hi, honey."

A coffee cup in his hand, her dad came out of the small kitchenette in the rear. "Isn't this a nice surprise?"

She gulped. "I hope you still feel that way after you hear what I've come to say."

Her mother put her hand to Lila's forehead. "Tell me you're not sick."

She stepped out of her reach. "No, Mom. It's not that."

Her father's face blanched. "Don't tell me that because of this sudden relationship with Sam..." His hand shook. Coffee dribbled down the sides of the mug. "That you're..."

She gasped. "No, Dad. Sam...me... He's been a perfect gentleman."

"Of course he has." Her mom smiled. "I think this is wonderful. Over the years, it was clear how sweet you were on him."

Her parents had known that she'd crushed on Sam Gibson during high school?

Lila's dad grabbed a couple of tissues to mop up the puddle forming on his desk. "To what do we owe the honor of your presence this afternoon?"

Better to just get it out than have them come up with further embarrassing speculations. Like what she was about to say wasn't embarrassing enough?

"Sam and I aren't engaged."

Lila steeled herself for their reaction.

Her mother put her arm around Lila's shoulder. "We know that, honey."

Her father snorted. "We may be boomers, but we know better than to believe everything on social media."

"You and Sam are dating, though, right?"

Deer in the headlights, she stared at her mom. In Truelove, dating was such an everybody-knows-your-business thing. Was that what she and Sam were doing? Dating?

"I think so…?" Her eyes darted between them. "But Aunt IdaLee and the matchmakers…"

"Say no more. We understand completely." Her mother waved her hand. "You two aren't the first couple caught in their schemes."

Her dad snorted. "Not even the first generation." He winked at her mom. "Nor the first to resort to a little romantic razzle-dazzle to throw those matchmaking bloodhounds off the scent."

"A fun little flimflam to distract and divert." Her mother fluttered her lashes. "But all came right in the end, didn't it, Clifford?"

Pushing his glasses up the bridge of his nose,

he grinned. "Why, yes, Myra Louise, I think it did." He planted a big kiss on her mom's mouth.

"Ugh. Stop." Making a face, Lila stepped back. "For the love of Monet. Please. I beg you." She blushed. "Anybody could walk in off the street and see you."

Her parents laughed. Lila groaned. This was why she'd grown up weird.

It was a moment ready-made for true confessions. But knowing how they viewed her art career, she wasn't yet ready to talk about California. If she wasn't awarded the position, no harm, no foul. And if she was…she'd cross that bridge when she had to.

The next days went by swiftly. She had a lot to accomplish before school let out for winter break next week. Every morning she hit the ground running.

She had to frame and mount her students' art projects before their parents came to the holiday assembly later in the week. She had projects of her own to finish, too. She'd promised several pieces for consignment to the upcoming Blue Ridge artisans' holiday festival in Asheville.

And she wasn't the only one playing catch-up. Sam, too. He and the crew were trying to finish the library renovation this week.

She and Sam texted each other periodically during various breaks in their day. But after spending the entire weekend in his company, she missed him. A lot.

Lila found herself drifting off in odd moments—like when she was supposed to be painting—thinking of him. And dreaming of when she'd see him again.

They did catch a late dinner at the pizza place on Tuesday. He'd stayed to finish a section of wall at the library. That evening, she'd closed out her last class at the rec center for the quarter.

She was so glad to see him, it was ridiculous. Like she hadn't seen him a mere forty-eight hours ago at the tree lighting.

He'd fallen into the habit of calling her before bedtime. All day she looked forward to his call and the chance to hear his voice. And every night, though she knew it was coming, when her cell rang, her pulse leaped.

Dropping whatever she was doing, she would grab for the phone. Her heart racing, she'd answer, trying to play it cool. But who was she kidding? She had it bad for Sam Gibson.

She found herself dreading the end of the week—and the end of her pretend engagement.

Midday on Friday, having just wrapped up the library project, Sam and his crew were stowing the last of their equipment in the van when his phone buzzed.

He glanced at the caller ID. "Guys." His heart thudded. "It's the real estate developer from Asheville."

Like the flipping of a switch, the jovial ribbing ceased. Deon, Neil and Rigo tensed. The next minutes would either be the start of fulfilling their dreams for their families.

Or sound the death knell, at least in the foreseeable future, to those hopes. Every one of the guys knew it. White painter's mask hanging around his neck, Neil's Adam's apple bobbed. Under the white painter's coverall, Deon squared his shoulders. Rigo gave him a thumbs-up.

God, no matter what, I trust You.

"Hello, Mr. Owens. Yes, sir?" His chest heaved. "Thank you, sir. Thank you so much." He grinned at the guys.

Eyes closed, lips moving in prayer, Deon slumped in relief. Rigo threw his arm around Neil's skinny shoulders.

"Please let me know what day next week you'd like me to swing by your office to sign the contact." He listened for a moment. "Thank you, sir, for your faith in Paint by the Numbers. We won't let you or your company down." He clicked off.

Deon let out a shout of thanksgiving. "Thank You, Lord."

"Group huddle!" Neil yelled.

And for a few, incredibly silly seconds, the four of them hugged it out. Sam felt almost dizzy with gratitude.

For a moment, it was like being on the football team again. After winning the state championship. But they'd won something far more powerful than a title. They'd won a life for their families. And he felt he'd earned back the respect his father had lost for the Gibson name.

Thank You, Father. When earthly fathers fail, You do not.

With no other job looming on the books, the four of them declared an early start to the weekend. They'd been waiting for this day for so long. Holding their collective breath.

Neil couldn't wait to take his pregnant wife to purchase the crib they'd been eyeing. Rigo decided to join his wife and surprise his kids at the school assembly. Deon called his girlfriend and made plans to take her out to dinner. Everyone headed out.

As for Sam?

There was only one person he couldn't wait to share his news with. Thanks to the school assembly, he reckoned Lila might find herself free for the rest of the day.

He was heading out tomorrow morning to bring Emma Cate home from her grandparents in Virginia. So he was still "engaged" for one more day. And he wanted to make the most of it.

Sam texted Lila. Hey, fiancée.

Little gray bubbles immediately popped up below his message. He could imagine her grin.

Hey, yourself. What r u doing? She texted back.

Thinking of u.

Wow, Gibson. You've upped your game this week.

He laughed. R u up for an adventure today?

More gray bubbles.

Every day is an adventure with u.

His mouth curved.

They agreed to meet at her house in fifteen minutes. He was there in ten. After she arrived, he made sure she had the proper coat and boots for hiking.

He held the door for her to slip into his truck. "There's a place I want to show you."

Shutting the door, he leaned across the open window. She gave him a sideways look. And his insides nosedived all the way to his boots. Did she not know how cute she was?

"Will I like this place?"

"I think so. There's a waterfall I want to show you."

"A waterfall in the mountains in December?"

"It's not far." He rubbed his jaw. "It's a special place to me. A place I think you'll appreciate."

She flipped her hair over her shoulder. "Okay, then. Let the adventure begin."

He had a feeling it already had. The day he'd climbed down a ladder. And a woman with gorgeous hair, wearing Christmas cat pajamas, had shouted at him for making too much racket.

It didn't take long to drive to the jumping-off point. On the trail, the snow was pristine and not too deep. Undisturbed except for deer prints.

As they hiked to the glen, their breath puffed in the wintry air.

When they emerged into the glade beneath the waterfall, she gasped. "Oh, Sam. It's beautiful." Pink mittens clasped under her chin, she did a slow 360. "I can't believe I've never been here before."

It was just as he'd imagined it would be here with her. The evergreens bedaubed with snow. The scarlet flash of a cardinal against the heavy-laden boughs. And other than the muted trickle of the falls, a hushed stillness. Like the glen had been waiting for her. For them.

"You're the only person I've brought here except for Emma Cate."

She went still. "Ever?"

"Ever."

Her eyes locked onto his. "Thank you."

"You're welcome." He stroked his chin. "I got good news today."

Her eyes grew large. "You got the Asheville contract?"

Sam grinned. "I did."

"That's fantastic." She threw her arms around him. "I'm so proud of you, Sam."

His arms circled her waist.

"Oh. Sorry." Her cheeks pinking, she lowered her arms from his neck. "I didn't mean to—"

"I'm picking up Emma Cate tomorrow morning."

She heaved a breath. "Right. I get it."

Keeping her in his arms, he didn't let her drift far.

"It's been fun, but I understand." Inching off her mitten, she held out her left hand. "You're asking for your rubber band back." Dropping her gaze, she attempted a smile but failed.

"Actually, no." Using the tip of his forefinger, he lifted her chin until her eyes met his again. "I was thinking I would tell Emma Cate we'll be seeing lots more of the wonderful Miss Penry." He gave her an uncertain look. "If you don't mind dating for real."

"I don't mind," she whispered.

He smiled at her. "Can I kiss you now?"

Lila smiled back. "Yes, please."

So he did.

Chapter Eleven

That weekend, Lila and Sam took Emma Cate to the ice-skating rink in Asheville. She and Sam each took one of her hands. Together, they did circles around the rink until Emma Cate's nose was practically blue, and Lila called it quits for the evening.

Even amid wrapping Christmas presents and decorating her tree on Sunday, there was little else in her thoughts except Sam and Emma Cate. Nor in her heart, either.

She hadn't known it was possible to be this happy.

The Head Start program always finished for the holidays a few days ahead of the rest of the school. Lila and Sam's mom worked out a schedule to watch Emma Cate during the day while Sam was at work and around Lila's remaining art classes.

Late Monday afternoon, Sam's mom had just finished her shift at the outlet mall and left with Emma Cate when Lila glanced out the window. The mailman pulled away from her mailbox on the street.

Bundled against the cold, she made a quick dash to the end of her drive. Her breath fogging in the air, she pulled out the mail and sorted through it. But as soon as she spied the return address on one envelope in particular, her hands began to shake.

Crushing the mail against her coat, she rushed to the house. Stomping the snow from her boots, she hurried inside. She leaned against the closed door, her chest heaving.

Had she been offered the artist-in-residence position? Or did the letter politely thank her for her interest but decline to offer her the grant?

Toeing out of her boots, she padded across the living room, shedding her coat and scarf as she headed into the kitchen. Trying to calm her frazzled nerves, she forced herself to examine the rest of the mail first. Christmas cards. A postcard from Paige on her honeymoon in tropical Hawaii. Bills.

Until only the letter with the California address stared up at her.

Okay. You can do this. She stared at the

creamy white envelope on the counter. *So go ahead. You can open it now.*

Still, she didn't make a move. *What are you waiting for? You've been waiting for this day for weeks.* Why couldn't she seem to make herself pick up the envelope?

Yes or no. Had she been passed over for other more qualified candidates? Either way, she'd finally know for sure.

The moment of truth. She grimaced. Not only about her art, but for the future course of her life. She'd come to a fork in the road of her dreams.

Deep breath. She inhaled. And prayed for the strength to accept the news, whether yea or nay.

Hand trembling, she reached for the letter. Slitting the flap with a butter knife, she then extracted the letter and unfolded it. Her eyes scanned the first line on the page.

The juried panel is pleased to offer the artist-in-residence position for the next calendar year to Lila Patricia Penry.

With a small cry, she fell against the counter. A validation of her hard work. Recognition of her talent. Acceptance. Affirmation. Approval.

Everything she'd longed for. What she'd been seeking her entire life. Tears rolled unchecked down her cheeks. They wanted her. They liked her. They got her.

Thank You, God. Thank You. She put her hand to her mouth. *This was You. All You.*

She did a crazy, happy dance in the middle of the kitchen. Laughing at herself, she read through the rest of the letter, which offered further details about the grant.

The stipend for living expenses was smaller than she'd anticipated. Her smile faded. The starving artist was not just a stereotype.

Yet the cost of living in California—housing, food, transportation—would be a great deal higher than it was in tiny Truelove. And the stipend was only a fraction of what she'd need on a monthly basis.

Lila would have to pay her own way to California. But apparently, learning from a master artist and becoming a part of the creative community was a reward in itself. And no one went into art to get rich.

In her head, she ran through the amount of money she had in her bank account. A lump settled in the base of her throat. It wouldn't be enough to sustain her for a year in California. She'd have to sell Granny's house to supplement her income.

All part of her original plan when she first applied for the position. The reason she'd wanted the house painted was for better resale value. But suddenly, California sunshine didn't hold the allure she once imagined it would.

Her gaze flitted around the kitchen, remembering the good times in this house. First with Granny. Then more recently with Sam and Emma Cate. She hadn't expected to feel such sadness at the prospect of leaving this place. The house had become home.

She ought to be ecstatic over this incredible news. This was a dream come true. Wasn't it?

Life was a series of choices. And being an adult meant recognizing each choice meant another choice couldn't be taken. But why would God finally give her this dream unless this was the road He wanted her to travel?

Feeling conflicted, she set the letter on the end of the island countertop. She had till Christmas to mull over her decision before the deadline to notify the committee. What was the right thing to do? Unlike a month ago, the answer was no longer as simple as she'd imagined.

In the space of a heartbeat, memories flooded her mind. Her mom and dad. Thanksgiving with Aunt IdaLee. Coffee with AnnaBeth. Ice skating with Emma Cate. Her eyes stung.

A kiss in the sleigh with Sam.

She had a lot to think about. She needed to weigh the pros and the cons. Decide what she truly wanted. Where she envisioned making a future for herself.

And who she wanted to be a part of her life.

That next afternoon, Sam left Truelove to head to Asheville. He had a meeting with the real estate developer to finalize contract details.

As he drove to the city, a light snow fell out of the pearl-gray sky. He turned on the radio to get the latest weather report but found himself instead listening to a local DJ's Christmas countdown favorites. Tapping his thumbs on the steering wheel to the music, he found himself humming along.

Yet another example of the Lila effect.

He smiled. He'd never met anyone who loved Christmas as much as she did. Other than Emma Cate, of course. Those two were a pair.

It had been the best week of his life. Being with Emma Cate and Lila felt right. Like they belonged together. Like a family.

The family he'd always dreamed of having. The kind of family he'd prayed for Emma Cate to know.

It amazed him how much the Penrys welcomed him into their fold. Considering his background, how much they seemed to genuinely like him. Even care for him and Emma Cate.

Their acceptance gave him hope he'd begun to

live down what his father had done. That there could be a future for him, Emma Cate and Lila.

His meeting took longer than he expected. Mr. Owens had gotten delayed at the job site. But once at the office, he and Sam quickly hammered out a production schedule.

The Paint by the Numbers crew would begin painting the first phase of homes the second week of January. After signing the contract, they shook hands. But in his truck, Sam realized it would be dinnertime before he reached Truelove.

Emma Cate had been over-the-moon ecstatic to learn they were going to be spending a lot more time with her beloved Miss Penry.

Yesterday Lila had seemed thrilled at the chance to be with Emma Cate. But this morning, Lila had appeared preoccupied when he dropped off Emma Cate. He hoped looking after his daughter hadn't been too much.

Lila had her own work to do, too. And he didn't want to take advantage of her good nature. The Christmas season was busy. But maybe he was overthinking it. Perhaps Lila was merely tired.

Sitting in the parking lot outside the real estate office, he sent off a quick text apologizing for his tardiness and to let Lila know his ETA.

No worries. Baking with EC. U like chocolate kiss cookies?

He typed, Yes.

One will b waiting 4 u.

He stuck his tongue in his cheek. A Lila kiss 2?

A millisecond ticked by until—I'll c what I can arrange.

He grinned.

Stashing his phone on the console, he headed out of Asheville. It was dark when he reached the turnoff on the highway to Truelove. But soon after, he passed the Truelove—Where True Love Awaits sign.

Funny how the sign used to semiannoy him. Now the sign made him think of Lila. The truck clattered over the bridge.

He drove down Main. The lights of the Christmas tree blazed out from the gazebo. Snow dusted the sidewalks around the square. Passing IdaLee's house, he pulled into Lila's driveway. He turned off the engine, but he made no move to get out.

For a second, he remained behind the wheel. Drinking in the sight of the little bungalow. Holding on a bit longer to the anticipation of seeing Emma Cate and Lila.

Through the open curtain, he glimpsed the twinkling lights of the Christmas tree he and Emma Cate had helped decorate in her living room. Upstairs and downstairs, white electric candles glowed from the windows.

Every single time he came here, he loved this house a little more. He felt like a weary traveler after a difficult journey. And Lila was the candle in the window welcoming him home.

Thank You for bringing her into my life and Emma Cate's.

Lila had come to mean far more to him than he'd ever imagined.

He made his way to the porch and climbed the steps. He was scraping the snow off his boots when Emma Cate threw open the door. She must have been watching.

"Daddy's here!" she called over her shoulder.

Lila appeared behind her. Maybe his daughter hadn't been the only one watching for him?

"Come inside." Lila beckoned. "Get out of the cold."

Inside the foyer, he toed out of his boots. Emma Cate held up her arms. Hoisting her up, he pressed his cold nose against her warm one.

She squealed. "Your face is too bristly, Daddy." She squirmed in his arms.

Laughing, he put her down.

She scampered toward the kitchen. "Time to eat, Daddy."

Lila smiled at him. "How about taking your coat off first?"

He unbuttoned his jacket. "Is my face too bristly for you?"

Cupping his jaw in her palm, she gave him a quick peck on his mouth. "Not at all."

He wrapped his arms around her shoulders. "I missed you."

"I missed you, too."

To his relief, whatever had been going on with her this morning, she appeared to be her sunny self once more.

He wound one of her curls around his index finger. "You and Emma Cate have fun today?"

She kissed him again. "Not as much fun without you."

He sniffed the aromas wafting from the kitchen. Vanilla, cinnamon sugar and Lila. His favorite flavors. "The house smells amazing. You smell amazing."

She cocked her head. "Flattery will so get you a meal at this house."

"What about the Lila kiss I was also promised?"

She planted her hands on her hips. "I just kissed you."

He touched her chin with his fingertip. "I think we can do better than that, don't you?"

"Daddy! Miss Penry!" Emma Cate called.

Lila's lips quirked. "Later."

Cradling the crown of her head, he kissed her forehead. "I'm going to hold you to that."

Dinner was a lively affair with Emma Cate

eager to tell him about how she and Lila had spent the day. A trip to the grocery store for baking supplies. And a visit out to the FieldStone ranch to cuddle Hunter's new litter of kittens.

Across the dinner table, Lila smiled at his daughter's exuberance. For the first time in his life, he felt truly happy. Utterly content. And he never wanted any of this to end.

Emma Cate climbed onto the stool at the island to draw on her sketchpad while he and Lila cleaned the kitchen.

Reluctantly, he called it a night. "Time to go, baby doll. Almost past your bedtime."

She rubbed her eyes. "Do we have to, Daddy? I like it here."

Oh, so did he. He wished he and Emma Cate never had to leave Lila or this house. The little girl slipped down from the stool.

Lila headed to the front hall to fetch their coats. "Get your book bag, Emma Cate."

He followed Lila to the door. "Don't forget your sketchpad."

Lila handed him his coat. Papers awry and sticking out of her book bag, Emma Cate joined them. He took hold of the bulging book bag. Crouching, Lila helped his daughter zip her puffy pink coat.

"What about de cookies, Miss Penry?"

"The cookies. You're exactly right." In one

graceful motion, Lila rose. "We can't forget the cookies." She ambled toward the kitchen. "Because if they stay here, I'll eat them."

Now thanks to the Asheville contract, his business looked to be secure. So maybe it was time to work on the rest of his future? He put on his coat. No maybe about it.

Lila returned with an aluminum-wrapped plate. Finally, he and Emma Cate were ready to head home. It wasn't home, though. Only the place where they slept. Hanging on to his leg, his daughter drooped against his side.

"I always forget what a production it is to get us out the door." Yet he couldn't resist lingering a moment more.

Lila leaned against the chair rail. "You forgot one more thing."

"What's that?"

"To kiss me good-night." She lifted her face. "Always kiss me good-night," she whispered.

He smiled. "My pleasure." Bending, he brushed his lips against hers.

"Sweet dreams."

He kissed her again. "They will be. Because I'll be dreaming of you."

She fluttered her lashes. "For a football jock, you're getting pretty good at the sweet nothings."

"What can I say? You inspire me." He grinned. "See you tomorrow."

The sweet look she gave him warmed him. All the way to the truck, through downtown, across the bridge, past the sign and to the trailer.

Emma Cate was quiet as he helped her into her blue flannel snowman pajamas. He tucked the covers around her and sat beside her on the bed to pray.

Afterward, she gave a great big yawn.

"Good night, my little hippopotamus." He tweaked the tip of her nose. "I love you." He reached for the switch on the bedside lamp.

"I love Miss Penry, Daddy." She yawned again. "Don't you?"

He froze. His heart thudded. Yes. Yes, he did.

"Daddy?"

He'd never said those words to anyone other than his mom and Emma Cate.

"Yes, baby doll," he whispered. "I love her, too."

But Emma Cate didn't hear. Her eyelashes brushing her cheeks, she was already fast asleep. Kissing her hair, he extinguished the light.

Out in the kitchen, he eyeballed the cookie plate he'd set on the counter. Perhaps one day in the not-too-distant future, Emma Cate would no longer call her beloved art teacher Miss Penry but instead call her... Mommy?

Snagging a chocolate kiss cookie, he ventured into the living room. Not anywhere near as good as a Lila kiss, but there was always tomorrow, right?

Grinning, he spotted Emma Cate's book bag lying on the couch where she'd left it. Papers poked out from every angle. He sighed. Maybe this week she'd learn some organization from Lila.

Sam recalled her upstairs studio. And then again, maybe not. His mouth curved. Perhaps the disorder was indicative of an artistic brain.

He dumped the contents of the book bag onto the couch beside him to sort and straighten. He set aside the sketchpad. Out of the disheveled batch of remaining papers, he removed a page with wide, dashed lines where she'd practiced writing "Emma Cate" over and over.

And on the bottom of the pile—*Wait. What's this?*

He held the official-looking, typed sheet closer to the lamp on the side table. The letterhead bore an address in California, and it had been sent to Lila.

Emma Cate must've accidentally picked it up off the counter with her sketchpad. He was setting it aside to return to Lila when "excited to have you join us in January" jumped out at him.

In California?

His gut jackknifed. What was this about? And though he had no business reading her mail, he couldn't help himself. With every sentence, his consternation grew.

Lila had been offered an artist-in-residence position at a prestigious university in California. He checked the date at the top. Why hadn't she told him?

Unless... His stomach tightened. She'd been trying to find a way to break the news to him. He checked the last paragraph. The deadline to let the university know her decision had been bolded.

When had she planned to tell him she was leaving Truelove? After she loaded her car? Before she pulled out of her driveway?

Feeling ill-used, he swept the pile of papers, including the letter, off the couch onto the floor. But just as quickly, his anger dissipated.

Betrayal wasn't in Lila's DNA. She was the most loyal person he'd ever known. Maybe she hadn't told him about the letter because she'd decided not to go to California.

Elation expanded inside his chest. She wasn't leaving. He'd never felt anything like what he felt for her. The way she looked at Emma Cate. The way she looked at him.

She wasn't faking. What had grown between them was real. And rare.

If she was staying in Truelove, it was because

she wanted to be with him and Emma Cate. That was the Lila he knew. The Lila he loved.

He raked his fingers through his hair. But was staying in Truelove the right thing for her? Every choice came at a cost. What was she losing by choosing them?

Jumping off the couch, he stepped over the papers on the rug and sat in front of his laptop at the kitchen table. He typed the name of the grant into the search engine. He brought up articles written by past winners. And read about the opportunities afforded them as a result of the grant.

Thirty minutes later, he had his answer. She'd chosen them over her art career. She'd be giving up everything she'd worked for. And for what? What did he have to offer her in return?

He slumped into the chair. Nothing. If he loved her... He took a ragged breath. If he really loved her, he couldn't allow her to make this sacrifice. Not for him.

Sam dropped his head into his hands.

It was a long night. Tossing and turning, he didn't get much sleep. Staring at the darkened ceiling of his bedroom, he wrestled through every scenario he could conceive. Searching for a happy resolution for all of them.

But bottom line, he had responsibilities in Truelove. Foremost to Emma Cate. Also to the guys.

He'd signed the contract with Owens. A contract with heavy fines should the crew not meet the developer's production schedule. The guys were depending on him to provide for their families. His life was here.

What about Lila's life? The rays of dawn's first light filtered through the gap in the curtain. Beautiful, talented Lila—he sucked in a shuddering breath—her life lay elsewhere.

If he truly loved her, he couldn't hold her back from achieving her dreams and everything God made her for. She was always and often to her own detriment putting others ahead of herself. But not this time.

His heart heavy, he rose and got dressed.

Once he heard Emma Cate stirring, he helped her get ready to leave. He fixed her cereal. But he didn't eat—couldn't eat. He felt sick to his stomach.

He was thankful that with Phil finally home for the holidays, his mother had volunteered to take care of Emma Cate today.

Sam texted Deon he might be late for work. On Monday, they'd started a new project—a rush job for the bank manager's wife, who'd decided at the last minute her interior walls needed a complete makeover before Christmas.

He made sure to bundle Emma Cate against the frigid temperatures. She raced ahead to the truck. As he stepped outside, the cold air blasted his cheeks. But it was nothing compared to how cold his heart felt.

Still in their pajamas and terry-cloth robes, Phil and his mom met them at the door. Giggling and dancing, Emma Cate pulled her Papa Phil into the living room to give him something she'd drawn for him last night. Sam and his mother stood alone together in the hall.

"Thanks, Mom, for watching Emma Cate today," he rasped. "I shouldn't be too late picking her up tonight." He put his hand on the doorknob.

She touched his coat sleeve. "What's wrong?"

He studied the toes of his boots. "Why do you think something's wrong?"

"No offense, honey. But you're looking rough this morning. Like you didn't get a wink of sleep."

He scrubbed his face. "I didn't."

"Did the deal in Asheville fall through?"

"No." He pinched his lips together. "That went forward as I'd anticipated."

Was it only twelve hours ago he'd felt on top of the world? Optimistic. Hopeful. His future full of promising possibilities.

"Don't shut me out, son." She took hold of his arm. "I'm here for you if you feel what's troubling you is something you want to share."

"It's the end, M-mom." His voice hitched. "Of everything I hoped."

Her face pinched. "Oh honey. What is it?"

Keeping his voice low, he gave her the condensed version of what he'd discovered last night. And the decision he'd made.

"Are you sure this is the way you want to handle things, Sam? If you and Lila were to talk this through..."

"It's the only thing I can do." He cast a look over her shoulder toward the living room. "Don't let on to Emma Cate. I want to be the one to tell her. Later tonight."

His mother shook her head. "I can't tell you how sorry I am about this, son. This breaks my heart for you and that little girl."

It was breaking his.

"What will you say to Lila?"

Sam shook his head. "I don't know, but somehow I've got to make her see sense. Her art is who she is. I won't stand in the way of her happiness. I have to ensure she doesn't miss out on this once-in-a-lifetime opportunity."

His mother tightened her belt robe. "And if you can't?"

"She has to leave Truelove." He took a jagged breath. "Even if I have to break her heart to make her go."

Chapter Twelve

Parked next to the curb outside IdaLee's, Sam clutched his cell.

Lila picked up on the first ring. "Hey, stranger."

He rubbed his forehead in a vain attempt to lessen the throbbing in his temple. "Are you up?"

"I am." She laughed. "I've even managed to get dressed and eat breakfast."

"Are you busy?"

"Not if it means I get to see you."

He winced.

"What did you have in mind?"

He turned the key in the ignition. "I need to talk to you." The engine purred. A curtain twitched aside at Miss IdaLee's front window.

"Can't stay away, huh?"

He could hear the smile in her voice.

"I thought I might drop by. If that was okay with you."

"More than okay. What time were you thinking?"

"I was thinking now." He put the truck in gear. "I'm pulling into your driveway."

She shrieked. "I don't have a speck of makeup on my face, Sam Gibson."

Through the phone, he heard the creak of the stairs.

"You couldn't have led with that?" A light came on in the upstairs window. "Give a girl a little warning, why don't you?"

There was the sound of a drawer yanked open.

"Lila?"

She would look gorgeous to him with or without makeup.

"Five minutes," she barked into the phone. "And not one minute before, buster." She clicked off.

Putting the truck in motion, he turned into her driveway and eased to a stop at the top. Turning off the engine, he sat there, gathering his courage. He let her have eight minutes, just to be sure. Throwing open the door, he climbed out like an old man.

Sam felt like an old man. A man whose best days were behind him. Her neighbor on the other side came out to retrieve his newspaper from the paper box. The woman across the street ventured out to walk her dog.

Boots crunching snow, he plowed up the steps.

He raised his hand to knock, but Lila threw open the door.

"Li—"

With a broad smile, she flung herself at him. Hands cupping his cheeks, she pressed her lips to his. "Good morning," she murmured against his mouth.

His lungs constricted. This couldn't happen.

Sam removed her hands from his face. "Stop."

Her eyes flickered.

Taking hold of her shoulders, he walked her back a step. Just so he could breathe. So he could think. So he wouldn't lose his nerve.

Her smile faltered. "What is it? Has something happened to Emma Cate?" Her eyes widened. "Tell me it's not—"

"Nothing's wrong with Emma Cate."

She blinked at the gruffness in his voice.

He hadn't meant for this to happen out here on the porch. But maybe it was better this way. No reason to prolong the agony for either of them. The sooner this business was ended between them, the better.

And he could rely on the ever-present Truelove grapevine to do the rest of his dirty work for him. The news of their very public breakup would be all over town within the hour.

"This is about us." He extricated the folded letter from inside his coat. "About this."

"I don't know what…" She took the letter from him and unfolded it. Her expression changed. "I—I can explain."

"You don't have to. Emma Cate grabbed it up with her stuff last night. I shouldn't have read it, but I did." He set his jaw. "I'm glad I did."

"I didn't tell you because it didn't matter." She crammed the letter in the pocket of her cardigan. "I promise you this means nothing."

Just as he'd feared.

She reached for him. But evading her hand, he stepped back. A sheen of tears glistened in her eyes. He'd wounded her. But if she touched him, he was lost already.

"It *is* important, Lila. In the art world, it's a career maker. The chance you've been waiting for."

"Suppose that turned out not to be what I was really waiting for, Sam?" Her gaze tremulous, she clasped her hands under her chin. "Suppose God has something so much bigger and better in store for us? More than we could have ever imagined?"

"Last night, the letter got me thinking about the future." He gestured between them. "Yours and mine."

She gave him a shy smile. "I've been thinking about the future, too."

"We don't have a future together, Lila."

Her hand went to her throat.

"We've been fooling ourselves." He laughed without mirth. "A Christmas dream from which it's time to awaken."

"No…"

She took hold of his coat, but he jerked free.

"What kind of future could there be?" He allowed a shade of scorn to roughen his voice. "Between someone like you and someone like me?"

She flinched.

"We've had fun. But now it's over. Time to move on. To head our separate ways. You had to know it could never be more for us."

"I don't believe that's all it was, Sam." Her mouth quivered. "That can't be all we've meant to each other. I love—"

"No!" He threw up his hands, warding off her words. There was no returning from that. "Don't make me say things to hurt you."

Her mouth pulled downward. "Whatever you're thinking, we can make it work."

"Are you hearing me at all, Lila?" He shook his head. "You had me pegged from the first. Commitment issues, remember? I realize now I'm more like my father than I supposed."

She frowned. "You're nothing like your father."

He shrugged. "I find it far easier to walk away than to stick around."

"You're lying." She thrust out her chin. "I'm

not sure why, but you're lying to me and to your-self."

"Stop making this worse than it has to be."

Panic started to set in. It was getting more difficult to fill his lungs with air. His despera-tion mounted.

How could he make her see this was for her own good? He refused to rob her of the chance for something when he only had himself to offer and nothing else. All the while fighting the deep-est longings of his heart.

Getting in his face, her gray-blue eyes went stormy. "You love me. I know you love me."

His heart seized. She'd left him no choice. One day, she'd thank him.

But right now, she was going to hate him. He hated himself for what he was about to say. And he prepared to do the hardest thing he'd ever done in his life. Push her away forever.

"Do I have to spell it out for you, Lila?" He grimaced. "I never thought you'd turn out to be like Courtney."

She staggered.

"I think you should go to California. There's no reason to stay in Truelove." He narrowed his eyes. "There's no one here to stay for."

Her face flamed. Her mouth opened and closed. Her eyes welled.

But having done the unforgivable, he turned

on his heel and walked away. Because as it turned out, he *was* far more like his father than he'd ever imagined.

Lila could do nothing but gape after him.

She remained frozen on the porch. Unable to move. Unable to speak. Unable to do anything but watch him back out of her drive and, with a screech of tires, peel away down the street.

Having said what he'd come to say, he couldn't wait to be rid of her. And she, the naive little idiot that she was, had never seen it coming.

Mrs. Desmond's Chihuahua barked from the sidewalk. Jerked out of her reverie, she winced at the pity in Mrs. Desmond's face. Slowly, she became aware Mrs. Desmond and her dog weren't the only ones who'd witnessed her complete humiliation.

Clutching the newspaper to his chest, Mr. Thompson stumbled up his driveway and disappeared into his house. She didn't have to turn her head in the other direction to guess her aunt IdaLee hadn't missed the early-morning spectacle, either.

In the heat of the moment, neither she nor Sam had bothered to lower their voices.

Shivering from more than the brisk, blowing wind, she wrapped her arms around herself. Tripping over her feet, she stumbled inside her house. Hands shaking, she shut the door against the cold.

Her beautiful, apple-green door.

Moisture flooded her eyes, blurring her vision. Pressing her shoulder blades against the panel, she slid to the floor. What had just happened out there? She pulled her knees to her chest.

What had she done to ruin everything growing between them? Or had she imagined feelings on his part that were never there? Eyes gushing, she dissolved into tears.

How could everything have gone so wrong since last night? The letter crinkled in her cardigan pocket. She squeezed her eyes shut. Anna-Beth had tried to warn her about secrets. About getting caught up in make-believe.

Perhaps Sam had been angry she hadn't told him about the residency position. Maybe he believed she'd used him.

But surely he didn't believe that of her. Surely he knew her better than that. Yet even as hurtful as his words had been, he hadn't seemed angry.

No, he'd been worse than angry. She sobbed into her hands. He'd sounded indifferent.

Reverting to high school, his barriers firmly in place. A shield around his thoughts and his heart. A wall where none had ever before existed between them. Erecting a barricade around himself. And completely shutting her out.

Why, God? Why did this happen?

Immediately, guilt smote her conscience.

After the choices she'd made—several of them highly questionable—*now* she'd finally decided to talk to God? When her plans had fallen to ashes. If only she'd sought His wisdom. But instead, she'd forged ahead, thinking she knew best. Determined to have her way.

If she'd turned to God first, she wouldn't have found herself in this heartbreaking mess. But the truth was, she hadn't wanted to hear what God had to say.

Like a willful child, she'd been full of her own plans. Heedless of the consequences. Rushing headlong into a disaster of her own making.

Because deep in her heart, she'd been afraid God wouldn't give her the answer she wanted. The art career. Sam and Emma Cate.

And rather than trusting Him to bring His best into her life, she'd taken the reins of her life into her own hands.

Her shoulders shook. Which didn't appear to be working out so well for her. Disobedience and rebellion never did.

I'm sorry, Father. Please forgive me for my foolishness. For my pride. Show me what You would have me do.

There was no immediate answer to her plea for guidance. She cried until there were no more tears left to cry. Regret and remorse flooded her heart.

Sam had shut her out. Like she'd shut her family out of her decision to apply for the residency program.

And then she had her answer. A direction. A place to start. She got off the floor.

Swiping the moisture off her cheeks, she found her coat and her purse. Putting her arm through the sleeve, her gaze caught on the green rubber band on her finger.

Her ribs ached. Removing the band, she dropped it inside the abyss of her purse. The place where dreams went to die.

In the garage, she let the motor warm before putting the car in gear. She backed out into the drive and pulled onto the deserted street.

She glanced at the dashboard clock. If she hurried, she could catch her parents as they arrived to start their day at the office.

Unlike Lila, her parents were early risers. They liked to start their day while the rest of Truelove was still enjoying their first cup of coffee. And early birds didn't only get the worm. They got first dibs on Main Street parking, too.

She was able to pull into a spot mere feet from their office. Steeling herself, she pulled open the glass-fronted door and stepped inside.

Putting away her purse in a desk drawer, her

mom smiled. "Hi, hon—" Her mother's smile dropped. "Cliff, get out here." Her voice rose. "Something's wrong with Lila."

"What?" Cup in hand, he rushed out of the small kitchenette. "Where?" He set the mug on the desk with a thud. "Lila?"

"I-I've got something to tell you. And I'm afraid you're going to be terribly disappointed in me." She tried to swallow past the boulder clogging her throat. "Again," she rasped.

Her father pulled her to the sofa in the reception area. She sank into the cushions, a parent on either side.

"I'm not sure where to begin." She knotted her hands. "I don't know how everything snowballed."

But she did know when everything had gotten out of control. From the moment she made a choice to keep secrets. When she made herself the ultimate authority on what was right for her.

She'd given her life to the Lord when she was Emma Cate's age. But over the last few months, she'd acted like it was hers to take back.

Her dad put his arm around her. "Starting at the beginning is usually the best way to proceed." The comforting scent of his aftershave enfolded her.

And she told them how different she'd always

felt from the other little girls. How she'd never quite fit into sleepy little Truelove.

Because of her hair. Because of the way she saw the world around her. Because of her passion for art.

How she never felt like she belonged. She told them about the grant. How she'd wanted to take her art to the next level.

To become a world-renowned artist. Surrounded by people who got her. Who understood her. How she was hoping to find her tribe in the glittering, vibrant art world on the Pacific coast.

"And I was wrong. So wrong. For keeping this from you. It's just…" She bit her lip. "I'm so sorry I've disappointed you again."

"You haven't disappointed us." Her mom's mouth quavered. "I'm sorry you felt you couldn't share the dearest part of your hopes and dreams with us."

Her father hugged her close. "Honestly, honey, we are so proud of you."

Lila's mother nodded. "Your talent. Your kind heart. Your creativity."

"Even if we didn't always know what to do with the beautiful little curly-haired gift God gave us." Her father sniffed. "We love you, Lila."

"Oh, Dad." She hugged them. "Mom. I love you both, too."

The three of them sat with their arms around each other for another few precious minutes.

"So have you decided to go to California?" Her mother folded her hands in her lap. "Because if you have, you have our full support."

Her dad wiped his finger under his glasses. "We want you to be true to yourself and happy."

But Lila wasn't sure she could be both.

She told them what happened with Sam that morning.

Her mother peered into her face. "Do you love him, Lila?"

"I—I do love him." She experienced a great sense of relief in finally saying the words out loud. "But he… He doesn't love me." She blinked her eyes furiously.

Her father rubbed his jaw. "I wouldn't be too sure about that. That Saturday before Thanksgiving when he showed us the finished paint job, I could see the way he looked at you. And the way you glowed."

She blushed.

Her dad smiled. "Which is exactly why I invited him to Thanksgiving dinner at Aunt IdaLee's."

Lila's mom patted her arm. "The Lord has great things in store for both of you."

"But are those great things in store for the both of us together?" she whispered. "Or apart?"

"I don't know, honey." Her mother found her

hand. "But I do know the best place to take our hurts, our confusion and our questions."

Lila nodded. For a short while, she'd forgotten. "I'll pray for God's best for Sam. No matter if God's best includes me or not."

Her dad kissed her cheek. "We'll pray, too."

"But know you're not alone." Her mother touched her cheek. "Your father and I are here for you."

Something else she'd forgotten. Despite her feelings to the contrary—and she was beginning to realize how truly deceptive feelings could be—she'd never been alone.

Lila had her family's love. And her heavenly Father's, too.

Chapter Thirteen

After work that night, Sam took Emma Cate to the drive-through for burgers.

"Miss Penry likes cheeseburgers, Daddy. Let's get her a milkshake, too."

Waiting his turn behind the vehicle at the intercom, he gripped the wheel. "We're not eating with her tonight."

Emma Cate poked out her lip. "But I didn't get to see her today. Don't you want to see her today?"

He had seen her today.

And he was pretty sure he was the last person on earth she'd want to see right now. If he lived to be a hundred, he'd never forget the look of utter betrayal on her features when he told her she should go to California.

The hardest words he'd ever said. That he and Emma Cate didn't need her. That there was nothing to keep her in Truelove. That's when he simply shut down.

So he'd just left her, standing on the porch. In the freezing cold. Staring after him. Her eyes welling. But that's why he'd left so fast.

Because he knew if he stayed one minute more, he'd never be able to walk away. If she said his name…if she cried…he'd be undone. Completely undone.

This was for the best. The best for Lila. Maybe if he kept saying that to himself he'd start believing it.

He was doing the right thing. The noble thing. *Aren't I, God?* But if that was true, why did the right, noble thing have to hurt so much?

After getting their food, he drove to the trailer while Emma Cate chattered away. Blissfully unaware he was about to shatter her world. His heart lay as heavy as a stone in his chest.

They ate their dinner at the little kitchenette. He didn't even try to eat. Emma Cate was full of plans for how she would spend her day with Lila tomorrow.

"Miss Penry's going to help me wrap my present for Mawmaw. And den we're going to…"

He wished this could've waited until after Christmas. But there was no help for it. What was done was done. And there was no use putting off the inevitable. No use avoiding it any longer.

"…tomorrow Miss Penry and I—"

"You're not going to see Miss Penry tomorrow, Emma Cate."

A tiny line creased her perfect brow. "Miss Penry is 'specting me, Daddy."

"There's been a change of plans." He leaned his elbows on the table. "Fact is, baby doll, neither one of us will be seeing Miss Penry anymore."

Her blue eyes widened. "No, Daddy. Dat's not right. We love Miss Penry."

Reaching, he pulled her into his lap. "I'm sorry. Miss Penry has a new job. And she's moving far away. She won't be your teacher anymore."

"No, Daddy. No." She shook her head so hard, little flyaway wisps of hair came out of her braids, hitting his face. "She wouldn't leave us. She wouldn't."

"Emma—"

"No!" Planting her small palms against his chest, she shoved him away and leaped to her feet. "Miss Penry loves us. We love Miss Penry."

Oh yes. His eyelids stung. So very much.

"I love Miss Penry, Daddy." Wailing, she collapsed into a small heap at his feet. "Don't let her go. Make her stay with us."

His heart nearly bursting in two, he gathered his daughter into his arms. The fight draining out of her, she let him hold her while she quietly sobbed.

Sam felt like sobbing. He was also angry. Not at Lila, but at himself.

What had he been thinking to allow someone to become important to his child? Her pain was his fault. The last two years he'd gone to such pains to ensure she—he—never became attached to anyone.

So she'd never suffer this kind of loss. The kind he'd suffered the day his father walked out never to return. Now his worst fears for Emma Cate were realized. And he had no one to blame but himself.

A difficult night turned into a bad morning. He was distracted. Unhappy. Why had he allowed Emma Cate to get so close to Lila?

The little girl kept asking him why Lila was leaving. Asking if she'd done something wrong. He tried to reassure her, but privately he asked himself the same question.

Had he done something wrong? Was he meant only for loneliness? Would there never be a happy ending for him?

Sam threw himself into the new job at the bank manager's house. But he made a lot of mistakes. Including ordering the wrong paint for the bank manager's sunroom.

In the living room, he tripped over a bucket of paint. Then a third of the way up the ladder in the master bedroom, he fell off. When he started painting the dining room the color selected for the kitchen, Deon sent him home.

Sam hadn't meant to drive past Lila's house. It wasn't on the way to anywhere. Kind of like his life. Yet somehow, without conscious thought, he found himself headed down her street.

Force of habit. A habit he needed to break. He hunched his shoulders. *Don't slow down. Don't hope to see her. Keep on moving.*

But when he spotted the For Sale sign, feeling sucker-punched, he hit the brakes. The sign made everything real. Rubbing raw the pain in his nerve endings.

She was leaving. He'd never see her again. The stupid hopes and dreams he'd only just begun to contemplate were shredded to pieces. Like his heart.

Idling in the middle of the street, he told himself to get moving again. That he'd get over her. That he and Emma Cate would be fine without her.

A blue sedan drove into Lila's driveway. He narrowed his eyes. The bungalow was dark. A woman in high-heeled boots got out of the car.

He wasn't sure where Lila was this morning. He hadn't talked with her since yesterday morning. He was clueless as to her whereabouts or her plans. And not talking to her was killing him.

An older couple got out of the sedan. The lady escorted the couple to the front porch. Whipping out a key, she let herself and the couple inside.

With a pang, he realized the woman was probably a Realtor. She was showing the house to prospective buyers. The idea of other people living in Lila's house gnawed at him like a physical ache.

Over the past month, he'd foolishly begun to imagine himself, Emma Cate and Lila here together.

The house had come to feel like home to him. The home he'd never had but always wanted. The home he'd envisioned making for Emma Cate.

Nestled under a mantle of snow, the cozy yellow house exuded sunshine. Like a promise of spring and good things to come. But not for him.

He found himself unable to swallow past the lump in his throat. He couldn't let this happen. He mustn't let this happen.

Sam might not be able to keep Lila in Truelove, but there was one thing he could do—prevent her house from falling into the hands of strangers.

With only one real estate agency in town, it

wasn't hard to find the online listing for the bungalow on his cell. Throwing the truck in motion, he headed toward the Truelove bank.

His jaw tight, he approached a teller. "Could you direct me to one of the bank officers?" He took a deep breath. "I'd like to get pre-approved for a home mortgage."

After Lila returned from talking with her parents, she'd emailed the committee and also contacted a local real estate agent. Her parents were naturally sad about her moving across the country but supportive of her pursuing her art.

She kept her own misgivings to herself. That night when she couldn't sleep, she'd stared at the ceiling above her bed. Taking out her memories of her time with Sam and Emma Cate one by one.

Pondering her reasons for leaving. Examining her reasons for wanting to stay. Yet at every turn, she remained torn, restless and conflicted.

And on Thursday morning when Mary Sue Ingersoll planted the For Sale sign in her yard, it felt as if she'd driven a stake through Lila's heart.

She was doing the right thing in taking the residency position in California. Wasn't she? But ever since she notified the committee of her acceptance, she'd second-guessed her decision.

Yet Sam had been so adamant about her not turning down this opportunity.

She'd been afraid to tell him about the offer. Foolishly, as it turned out. He didn't care if she left or not. He'd been crystal clear about nothing keeping her in Truelove.

Lying on the couch Friday, Lila paged through her phone. With school out for the holidays, she'd been doing a lot of lying around since Wednesday. Doing much of nothing. Contemplating the last month. Her future.

Good thing she'd turned in the landscapes to the arts festival last week. And for the first time in her life, she had no desire to draw or paint or create. She'd never felt more unlike herself in her life.

Or as lonely. It was an alarming to not feel like herself. To feel only this great, gaping sadness.

With the house on the market, soon she would indeed be on her way. But was that what she wanted? She needed the house to sell to finance her relocation.

Perhaps, though, the house wouldn't sell. She brightened. And her decision to go or stay would be made for her.

The cell rang in her hands. Jolting, she fumbled the phone. Making a quick save, she clicked On.

"Oh, Mary Sue, hi." She pressed the phone

to her ear. Her stomach plummeted at the real estate agent's news. "Someone's made an offer already?"

Her house had been on the market for less than two days. Mary Sue had shown the house twice on Thursday. And Lila had made herself scarce.

"They offered full price."

She could hear the smile in Mary Sue's voice.

"Very smart of you to get it spruced up with new paint before listing it."

Not so smart to get her heart entangled by a certain paint contractor and his little girl. And she'd not foreseen the house selling almost immediately, further complicating her feelings.

"Lila, are you still there?" Mary Sue's voice lowered. "I thought you'd be pleased."

She ought to be happy. Thrilled. But she wasn't. Not even a smidgen.

"Was the buyer the retirees or the divorced mom?"

"Neither." Mary Sue laughed. "A young family put in a bid, sight unseen."

A young family. But not hers. She pushed aside dreams of summer afternoons on the porch. Of drinking sweet tea with a blond former quarterback. Of watching Emma Cate run through sprinklers in her swimsuit. Of birthday parties, celebrations and anniversaries that would never be.

"Will you accept their offer, Lila? I told the buyer I'd call him ASAP with your decision."

So this was really going to happen. No turning back. It would be strange seeing another family in her grandmother's house. Although she wouldn't be here to see it. A blessing in disguise.

"I accept their offer. I just h-hope…" Emotion clogged her throat. "I just hope their family will be as happy in this house as my family has been."

"The buyer was pre-approved for a loan. Once I give him the go-ahead, the terms of the contract will be set in motion."

Mary Sue went on to explain the details of closing, but Lila had a hard time taking in everything she said. Her temples throbbed. Her heart ached. She put a hand to her head.

This was the beginning of the end. She wouldn't be here for the first crocus to burst forth through the snow. She wouldn't get to read stories with Emma Cate anymore. She'd never kiss Sam again.

Mary Sue droned on and on. The buyer had requested to close the first week in January. Which would work with Lila's timetable. She had to be in California by the eighth. It was all happening so fast.

Lila wanted to weep. She wanted to scream. She wanted Sam. And Emma Cate. She wanted to share a life with them.

"You can handle everything, right?" She became desperate to get off the phone before she totally disgraced herself. Before she totally lost it. "I have to go. Now."

"Oh…okay…" A note of confusion laced Mary Sue's voice. "Are you sure you're feeling all right, Lila honey?"

She didn't trust herself to speak.

"If you're having second thoughts about selling the house…"

Second thoughts? Fifth, tenth and twelfth thoughts.

"This isn't a done deal, sweetie. Not yet. If you'd rather think about—"

"No." The last thing on earth she wanted to do was think anymore. That's all she'd been doing. "It's fine. I'm fine. Start the paperwork, Mary Sue."

A beat of silence.

"If you're sure…"

Lila gulped. "I'm sure," she whispered. And she was.

Sure she was making the biggest mistake of her life. And she wasn't only thinking about the house. Yet what other choice did she have? Sam didn't want her in his life.

That afternoon, she emailed her resignation to the school principal, Mrs. Stallings. Canceled next semester's art classes at the rec center.

In a big show of solidarity, her dad and mom arranged to shut down their own business the week of her move to help her drive the moving van and get established in her new digs. A tremendous sacrifice on their part.

For accountants, the start of the new year meant the start of tax season. Their busiest time of year. But they were so endearingly committed to helping her succeed. Every time she thought about their love and support, she had to sit down for a cry.

Which she was doing a lot of anyway.

Over the weekend, AnnaBeth, her mom and dad offered to help her start packing, but she preferred to do her mourning alone. As she packed her belongings, many of them Granny's, that's exactly what it felt like—grieving. Saying goodbye to the past, the present. And most painful of all, a future that was never meant to be.

Every room in the house contained so many memories. Baking cookies in the kitchen with Emma Cate. Laughing with Sam in the living room. Strangely, the art studio was the one room she found easiest to tear down.

Where once she'd experienced this driving passion to capture the world on canvas, now she felt only a numbing emptiness. Like missing an amputated limb. In its place was only aching sadness and loss.

The loss of something so vital, so consuming, scared her. She'd lost her inspiration. Her muse. Her heart.

She'd stopped seeing the color. That was what frightened her the most. The world had receded into a blend of white and gray shadows.

And when she found herself in the glittering world she'd fought so hard to become part of, what then?

She wondered, if even then, she'd ever recover what she'd lost. The thing that made her art. The thing inside that made her Lila.

Maybe she'd forever lost herself.

She spent a lot of time in prayer. Sustaining her through the dark days and nights of uncertainty. *God, will this ever get better? Help me, Father. Help me to—*

She grabbed her ringing phone. "Hello?"

"I've made a big pot of vegetable beef soup."

"Aunt IdaLee?"

"I'd love for you to come and share it with me."

She glanced around the kitchen. At the open cabinets. The half-empty shelves. The boxes waiting to be filled. It was December twenty-third.

But on this gloomy, overcast day, comfort food sounded like bliss. After a slow start, winter had arrived with a vengeance and settled in for the duration. Yet another snowfall was forecast for Christmas Eve.

This could be the last time she had the chance to have lunch with her great-aunt. IdaLee would miss her company. But not as much as she'd miss her aunt IdaLee.

Lila bit her lip to keep it from wobbling. "I'll be there in a few minutes, Aunt IdaLee."

"Wonderful. See you soon."

Donning her coat, she slipped out of the house and cut across the backyard to the Victorian. Her aunt's wrinkled face lifted at the sight of her. Lila concentrated on not breaking down entirely. She really had to stop losing it at the slightest provocation.

Aunt IdaLee ushered her into the cheerful, old-fashioned kitchen. She was wearing her lavender velour tracksuit—her aunt must have been to the rec center for the Silver Sneakers exercise class that morning.

While they ate at the kitchen table, IdaLee kept the conversation light. Which Lila appreciated. Her aunt spoke of Christmas cards she'd received from former students. Lunch with the Double Name Club tomorrow. And the upcoming Christmas Eve service.

Suddenly, Lila didn't feel like eating. An all-too-common occurrence these days. She put down her spoon. "I'll have to find a new church home, too."

A silence fell. Broken only by the ticking of the grandfather clock in the front parlor.

"I thought you'd be happy about your new life in California."

She kept her gaze trained on the rim of her bowl. "So did I," she whispered.

"A dream come true."

Was that what it was? A dream come true. Or was it a case of wishing for the moon and, upon receiving it, wondering what she'd ever wanted with the moon in the first place?

"You were always different from the other children."

She folded her napkin in her lap. "I remember you saying that to Mom."

"I think you misunderstood what I meant." The old woman leaned her shoulder blades against the slats of the chair. "I meant you were different in the most wonderfully, unique way. That's why I convinced your parents to let you go that summer to the NC School of the Arts program for gifted children."

Her gaze shot up. "That was you?" Something tight inside her loosened.

That was the summer she began to paint what she saw and felt.

"It's perfectly normal for dreams to change

and evolve as we change and evolve." Her aunt placed her gnarled hands flat on the tabletop. "It's also perfectly acceptable to have more than one dream."

Dropping her gaze, Lila pleated the edge of her napkin.

"Are you sure moving away is what you want, dear heart?"

"Perhaps some dreams aren't meant to be." She folded and refolded her napkin. "Without Sam and Emma Cate…" She swallowed. "There's no reason to stay in Truelove."

"But if you leave your heart behind, what good will it do to go to California?"

"I don't know." She blinked rapidly. "It seems in losing Sam, I've lost both dreams, Aunt IdaLee."

Shame clawed at her throat. Her parents weren't the only ones to whom she owed an apology.

"I'm sorry for allowing you to think we were… more than what we actually were, Aunt IdaLee." She swallowed. "I'm sorry for messing up your plans for Sam and the special woman you picked out for him."

The old woman laughed. "The special woman is you, Lila Pat." Her aunt's thin shoulders shook. "Who do you think convinced your father the house needed painting in the first place? Who do you think urged him to get an estimate from Paint by the Numbers and a certain Samuel Gibson?"

Lila gaped. "You believed *I* was the perfect woman for him?"

"And he's the perfect man for you." IdaLee gave her a sly look. "I figured it was time to take action. You'd pined over that young man long enough."

Lila threw out her hands. "Does absolutely *everyone* in Truelove know what a fool I made of myself over him in high school?"

Her aunt's lips twitched. "Everyone except him."

"So you and the matchmakers still think Sam and I are the perfect match for each other?"

IdaLee smiled. "We do."

She made a face. "You must have me confused with somebody else."

"I see you perfectly, Lila Pat. And what I see is beautiful. As does your Creator."

She sighed. "A beautiful mess."

"You must learn to see your worth in God's sight. You're His beloved child. When He looks at you, He sees someone worth dying for. Worth loving."

Lila dropped her eyes.

"Stop listening to the voices speaking lies about who you truly are."

Her head snapped up. How had her aunt known?

"Listen to what God says about you. He calls you Mine. You are His beloved child." She wagged her bony finger. "Give no place to those other lies."

Suddenly it occurred to Lila it had been a while since she'd listened to—given space to—the Courtney voice. She had no doubt God had used Sam in her life to help her silence those lies.

"I'm trying to change my understanding of how God sees me. But I'm not there yet."

Her aunt nodded. "It's often a slow process to change the way we think about ourselves. Perhaps a lifetime's work. To undo the negative thought patterns we've allowed to take root. But God is faithful." The old woman's face gentled. "And above all, God is good. Never, never forget that."

She released a slow trickle of air from between her lips. "What should I do, Aunt IdaLee? Should I go or stay?"

"Only you can make that decision. And with the Lord's help."

Gathering her hair off her shoulders, she wrapped the ends into a ball around her fist. "I know it shows a lack of faith, but I keep asking God for a sign."

"I'm not so sure about that. The Lord graciously gave Gideon a fleece. Yet it was still up to Gideon to choose in faith to believe. And so I think it is for you. Which is why I have a gift under the Christmas tree for you today."

Her never-married, childless great-aunt was renowned for somehow always knowing what each of her nieces and nephews wanted for Christmas. Things they weren't aware they wanted or needed until they opened Aunt IdaLee's gift.

Lila frowned. "But you always give us our gifts on Christmas Eve."

"Today is the day you get your gift."

Her aunt pushed away from the table, and Lila followed her into the front parlor. The tangy scent of evergreen permeated the room.

Aglow on the top of the tree, the star pushed back the shadows to the corners of the room. Remembering the look of wonder on Emma Cate's face as she placed the star there, Lila's heart caught in her throat.

That had been a day of new beginnings. The day Emma Cate's Daddy Sam officially became her forever daddy. And the day he first began to open his heart to Lila.

In front of the tree, her aunt held out her hands for Lila to grasp hold. Her skin felt paper thin to Lila's touch. Yet in the blaze of the multicolored strands of light, IdaLee's violet-blue eyes gleamed. Her elderly aunt's body might appear frail, but her spirit and her faith were indomitable.

"Secrets breed misunderstanding, but truth brings illumination. And so my gift to you this year is truth."

Lila tilted her head. "I don't understand."

"You should know the truth behind who's buying your house."

She stared at her aunt. "My house?"

IdaLee kept a firm grip on her hands. "Sam is buying your house."

Lila's brow creased. "Why?"

"Because he and Emma Cate love that house. Because he loves you." Her aunt's snowy-white hair reflected silver in the lights of the tree. "But he refuses to take something—*you*—in exchange for nothing—*himself*."

She stiffened. "Sam Gibson isn't nothing."

"You're preaching to the choir." IdaLee squeezed her hands. "Though he refused to keep you from your dreams, he couldn't help keeping one thing about you close."

"So he's buying my house," she whispered.

"I believe the best decisions are made when you are in possession of all the facts." Her aunt touched Lila's cheek. "It's up to you to choose whether to believe or not. With the Lord's guidance, choose wisely, dear Lila Pat."

Throughout the rest of what remained of the day, she wrestled with what to do. With what the Lord would have her do.

After a long, sleepless night, she rose to greet the dawn of Christmas Eve. Snow had once again fallen during the night. Needing a change of scenery, she drove down Main, across the bridge, past the welcome sign to the promontory beyond the rec center.

Parking in the gravel lot, she got out. Heavily bundled against the cold in her knit cap, coat, boots and mittens, she brushed the snow off the giant granite boulder. She sat down to think and pray.

Remaining in Truelove could open herself to a new world of hurt. Sam had been clear that he didn't love her. Eventually, though, he would move past his fears and insecurities.

He'd meet someone. Someone he'd love enough to drop his barriers. Lower his shield. Remove the barricade around his heart.

And by staying in small, sleepy Truelove, she'd have a front-row seat to watch him fall in love with someone else. She'd have an up close and personal opportunity to witness someone else mother Emma Cate.

She fisted her gloves in her lap. Emma Cate needed a mother. Sam needed someone to love.

But oh, how I wish, dear God, it could have been me.

And what about her art?

Sleepy, beautiful Truelove winked below her perch on the outcrop. Her heart slowed. She had a bird's-eye view. And once again, the colors sprang to life.

Like a holiday ribbon, the silvery flash of the

river curled in a horseshoe around the town. Stoplights glowed red and green on Main. White lights twinkled from the gazebo on the square. Tiny cars and humans went about their usual morning business.

Beyond the town, the smoky indigo smudge of mountains undulated on the horizon. Warming rays from a pale sun steadily climbed the ridges. Lifting the shadows. Bathing the world, her world, in a fresh garment of light.

And then she knew. She just knew. This wasn't the right time to leave Truelove.

She wasn't ready to leave this place. Her art wasn't ready. She might never be ready.

But that would be okay. Peace whispered through her heart. More than okay.

It was here she'd discovered her passion. It was here she saw the colors. It was this place the Lord had gifted her to create.

So many techniques to yet explore. So many landscapes in her Blue Ridge mountain home yet to capture. And it was good. So very, very good.

Because God was good.

For the first time in days, she felt the call to put paint onto canvas.

Lila got off the rock.

She didn't have a place to live anymore. She didn't have a job. Although she had a feeling Mrs. Stallings, would take her back in a heartbeat.

The rec center would be thrilled to reschedule her evening classes. More commissions would come. The Lord would provide.

She could trust Him to guide her to the next thing He had for her. On the path of life, He'd shine a spotlight on her next step, but probably no more than one step at a time. Because that was what it meant to walk in faith.

Returning to her car, she felt a lightness. The weight of responsibility to be the ruler of her life had been lifted from her shoulders. A weight she was never meant to bear.

At the house, she dug through the box containing her art materials. She could hardly wait to start a new project. But she took out only what she needed. She'd still need to pack up the rest of the house.

Phone calls would need to be made. A call to her wonderful parents. And a call to the California university, declining their gracious invitation. But first on her list? She hit speed dial.

"Aunt IdaLee, how would you feel about renting me a room?"

Whether Sam loved her or not, what she truly wanted was to remain in Truelove. To be closer to everyone, including Emma Cate and Sam, that she loved the most.

Chapter Fourteen

A few hours after getting off the phone with her aunt and then her parents, Lila received an unexpected call from Margary Jenkins, the head of the holiday arts festival in Asheville. Mrs. Jenkins was a very important person in the Blue Ridge Artisan Guild and art circles throughout the Southeast.

"Your paintings stole the show last weekend, Miss Penry. And we had a record turnout."

"I'm so glad the weekend was a success, Mrs. Jenkins."

Lila continued to box the shelf of books beside the fireplace in her living room. She hoped to finish packing the bookcases before her family gathered at Aunt IdaLee's house that evening to celebrate Christmas Eve together.

"I understand you turned down the Faraday grant."

She sank onto the ottoman. "Yes, that's right."

How did Mrs. Jenkins know that?

"I wondered if you'd tell me why."

Frowning, she ran her tongue over her dry lips. Mrs. Jenkins and her husband, Garland, were wealthy patrons of the arts. Very powerful. Very influential.

"I decided the grant wasn't a good fit for me. My heart and my art lie closer to home. Because these mountains are my home. In my blood. And I decided there was enough here to attempt to capture for a lifetime."

Was she about to be blackballed by the entire East Coast art community?

"That's what my friend said you'd told the committee." Mrs. Jenkins paused. "Did I mention Lola Faraday, the widow of Worth Faraday, and I were roommates at Ashmont College together?"

Lila closed her eyes. This was bad. Very bad.

"No, ma'am," she whispered. "I don't believe you did."

The small liberal arts college had a wonderful reputation. About forty minutes north of Truelove, the college was known for its music program. It had produced some prominent folk singers, continuing a rich Appalachian ballad heritage.

"Garland, Lola and I grew up in the Blue

Ridge. Not too far from your Truelove mountain home. There is something in your work, Miss Penry." The woman's voice hitched. "Some indefinable essence that quite touches the soul."

Lila slid down to the rug. "Thank you, ma'am," she managed to rasp.

"It has long been our desire to establish a grant at our alma mater for an artist-in-residence position. And not only provide the resources and freedom for the artist to broaden her scope, but to also help us create a visual arts program that will become a center for creative exploration throughout the nation."

"Th-that sounds incredibly exciting."

Mrs. Jenkins laughed. "I should hope so, because we'd like to ask you to become our artist in residence."

Lila gasped. "Me? Mrs. Jenkins, I am so flattered. But you realize that I don't have a PhD. And I'm only—"

"You are astonishingly gifted. Your youth is a plus in our book. As is your fresh, out-of-the-box approach. Art is about innovation. We see you as a brisk wind of change. We trust your instincts and plan to leave the development of the program in your capable hands."

The woman named a salary that almost blew off Lila's Christmas puppy socks.

"You do understand, of course, that this is not

just a one-year residency. I hope you will come to love our campus and the exciting work to which we're committed and that you will consider staying on indefinitely."

Lila's heart pounded. Was this really happening? They wanted her? They really wanted her? But she thought about her work with young artists like Emma Cate.

"A great deal of my inspiration, Mrs. Jenkins, comes from my work with the children in Truelove."

"Part our vision is for you to bring master artists from every medium onto the faculty. In addition to establishing various bachelor of fine arts degrees, we envision offering these programs at a reduced rate for the children in the surrounding region. To inspire future generations of artists. Will you accept our offer, Miss Penry?"

If she'd learned anything over the last weeks, it was to not rush down a path she wasn't first sure the Lord intended.

"Can I pray over this decision, Mrs. Jenkins, and let you know after Christmas?"

"Why, yes." The woman's voice gentled. "I look forward to hearing your decision. And just so you know, I'll be saying a few prayers of my own." She chuckled. "Happy Christmas Eve, Miss Penry."

"Thank you so much, Mrs. Jenkins. Merry Christmas to you, too."

Clicking off, Lila waited for the shock to wear off before she made any attempt to get to her feet.

"Lord, is this You?" she whispered.

Where had this out-of-the-blue, close-to-home, more-than-she-could've-ever-conceived-or-imagined dream offer come from but from Him?

Getting on her knees, she clasped her hands under her chin. "So what do You think?"

The best of both worlds. Combining her passion to create with her passion to nurture. And she could commute from home. If she had a home, that is.

"Please don't let me get all excited if this isn't Your desire for me." She cleared her throat. "But no matter what, I choose You, God. I choose You."

And although it was the middle of the day, she lay on the couch to listen and pray. Then out of sheer exhaustion, she fell asleep.

When she awoke, she could tell from the longer shadows on the living room wall, several hours had passed. It must be late afternoon.

But immediately, she felt a sense of peace. And somehow she knew this time His answer about the artist-in-residence position at Ashmont was yes.

Tears welled in her eyes. Aunt IdaLee was right. About everything.

God was faithful. And He was good. So very, very good.

Late that afternoon, Sam was walking out of the paint store when his cell rang. He deposited the tins in his pickup and dug his phone out of his pocket. Seeing IdaLee Moore on the caller ID, his stomach tanked.

"Would you mind coming by the house, Samuel? I have a gift for Emma Cate."

Mind?

He'd rather walk barefoot over finishing nails, but Miss IdaLee had been so kind to Emma Cate. And though he was aware the old woman probably intended to give him a good talking-to, he couldn't find it in his heart to refuse her.

Actually, these last few days he didn't have the heart to fight much of anything.

"Sure, Miss IdaLee." He glanced at the time. "Give me ten minutes and I'll be there."

The old lady must have been watching for him, because she had the door open and stood waiting for him before he was halfway up the porch steps.

IdaLee ushered him through the door. "I hear congratulations are in order."

Scraping his feet on the mat to make sure he

didn't track any snow inside, he followed the diminutive octogenarian toward the living room. "We start phase one of the Asheville development project after New Year's. It's a huge blessing for Paint by the Numbers."

He was careful to keep his gaze averted from the Christmas tree. But memories of decorating the tree with Lila and her family weren't as easily averted. In contrast, he and Emma Cate would keep a quiet Christmas Eve with his folks. She and his mother were even now baking gingerbread cookies to leave for Santa.

"I wasn't talking about your new contract." The old woman sank into the green wing-back chair by the fire. "Take a seat." She gestured toward the sofa. "I hear we're going to be neighbors. Welcome to the neighborhood."

He leaned forward. "I hope you don't mind that I bought your sister's house, Miss IdaLee."

"I'd hoped you and Emma Cate would join Lila in becoming my neighbors."

He had hoped so, too.

Sam swallowed. "Some things aren't meant to be."

"Have you told her how you feel?"

"I don't—"

"Stop lying to yourself, Samuel. I've seen how you look at her when you think no one else is watching."

He knotted his hands together. "It doesn't matter how I feel, Miss IdaLee."

"Of course it matters." The old lady squared her shoulders. "She's in love with you."

His gut twisted. "But even if that were true, all the more reason for her to go."

IdaLee gripped the armrests. "What are you talking about?"

"She's meant for better things. She deserves more than me, the son of a swindler."

"You're talking nonsense."

"No, ma'am." He shook his head. "Her art is an expression of who she is. I love the way she is, and I would never do anything to keep her from this opportunity."

"Lila is more than her art."

"I won't hold her back from following her dream." He jutted his jaw. "I won't take something from her when I have nothing to offer her in comparison."

The retired schoolteacher wagged her bony finger at him. "That stubborn pride of yours is going to cost you everything. You are everything that she wants, you foolish boy."

"I wish…"

What did it matter what he wished?

He rested his elbows on his knees. "It's better this way." A thickness clogged his throat. He lumbered to his feet. "I—I need to go. You have family coming over soon."

Planting her palms on the armrests, the old woman rose. "Let me get that gift for Emma Cate." She stooped to retrieve a present from under the tree. Tied around the brown parcel package was a shiny gold ribbon.

"Thank you, Miss IdaLee, for thinking of Emma Cate this Christmas. Happy Christmas Eve."

"Samuel—"

"I've got to go, ma'am."

Clutching the gift under his arm, he rushed out of IdaLee's parlor and onto the porch. Almost against his will, his gaze was drawn to the house next door.

The closing was nine days away. And after that, Lila would leave Truelove. Probably forever.

And he'd never see her again.

Shuttered and dark, Lila's house—his house—had a forlorn air. His heart skipped a beat.

Perhaps she was already gone.

His legs gave out from under him. And he sank down heavily on the bottom step. Porch planks creaked behind him followed by the old lady's slow, shuffling gait.

"You rushed out of there before I had a chance to give you your gift."

Heartsick, he dropped his head. "You don't need to give me a present, Miss IdaLee."

"I know I don't *need* to give anybody a gift, Samuel Gibson, but I do so because I want to. Now stand up and take your gift like a man," she snapped. "'Cause I'm too old and rickety to be sitting on that cold step."

He jerked to his feet. Everyone in Truelove from eight to eighty with a lick of sense knew better than to cross Miss IdaLee when she used that schoolteacher voice. He came up onto the porch again.

"I had to grab my coat." She wound a scarf around her neck. "You young folks don't mind the cold the way these old bones of mine do."

"Yes, ma'am." Another trick he'd learned at school—when called on the carpet, stick to polite, vague phrases.

She narrowed her eyes at him. "You're probably noticing I don't have anything in my hands."

He had noticed that, but he was smart enough not to bring it up. "Yes, ma'am."

A smile teased the corner of her lips. "You were the handsomest little boy I ever taught. And always knew just the right way to charm." She made a face. "But I'm not senile yet."

"No, ma'am."

She laughed. "You two are going to be the death of me, Samuel Gibson."

He touched her arm, all joking aside. "No, ma'am. You'll outlive us all."

"Don't think I won't. Just to spite you." She straightened her thin shoulders. "Here's my gift to you. Two gifts, actually. To see yourself the way everyone else in this town sees you. I give you the gift of respect you've already earned..."

Hands clenching at his side, his eyes stung.

"...and the gift of a second chance. Don't waste it."

He swallowed, hard.

"Your second chance is that Lila has decided to stay in Truelove." IdaLee smiled. "Probably right here in this very house. Unless you can offer her a better..." She crooked her eyebrow. "...deal."

There was a glint of steel in her violet eyes. And he knew right then and there that their little pretend engagement had fooled no one. Least of all Miss IdaLee Moore.

"Don't leave it too late, dear heart." Her eyes grew moist. "It's the words unspoken you'll regret the most. Not many people know this, but there was a young man I loved..." She turned her face away.

"Miss IdaLee?"

"I'm sure you can hardly imagine that an old, dried-up spinster like me was once young and fair, but I was."

He clasped her gnarled, blue-veined hand.

"I let pride and hurt feelings and fear..." She blinked away tears. "I waited too long. We lost each other."

His heart thumped painfully.

She squeezed his hand. "Don't be as foolish as we were, Samuel. Or you'll spend the rest of your life mourning what could have been. Tell Lila what's in your heart. Give her the respect of allowing her to make her own choices."

It felt as if his heart was near to bursting.

"Well, go on now." She gave him a little shove. "I'm not going to stand out here all afternoon in this weather. I'm expecting company tonight."

A sudden idea struck him.

"How would you feel about more company than usual this Christmas Eve, Miss IdaLee?"

"I'd say the more the merrier." She smiled. "What do you have in mind?"

He outlined his plan to bring Lila's friends and family together at IdaLee's a little earlier than the old woman's usual Christmas Eve gathering.

"I figure since I broke up with Lila in public, she at least deserves as public a proposal." He sighed. "Or I'll give her the chance to just as publicly reject me."

Lila's aunt rolled her eyes. "Not going to happen. I'll make some calls. Get everyone here."

"I appreciate that, Miss IdaLee. I would like

to call Mr. and Mrs. Penry myself. I want to do this the right way. No more secrets."

"Let me put Emma Cate's gift back under the tree." The old woman winked at him. "I can give it to her myself later."

Miss IdaLee went inside to make her calls and, too nervous to do anything but pace, Sam called Lila's parents.

With both of them on the line, he apologized for hurting their daughter, told them he'd like to propose to Lila tonight and asked for their blessing. Which they readily gave. They were delighted and promised to arrive within the hour.

"You're going to call your mother and let her in on it, too, aren't you?" Mrs. Penry asked.

"She's my next call."

"Wonderful." Mr. Penry's voice hitched. "Welcome to the family, son."

He wished he were as sure as her dad that Lila would forgive him and say yes.

"We'll see you soon at Aunt IdaLee's."

His mom was next. At his news, her joyful shriek for Phil to get on the other line nearly deafened him. He'd no sooner gotten off the phone with them when a bevy of trucks, SUVs and sedans pulled up to the curb outside the Victorian.

The little general, IdaLee Moore, was nothing if not efficient.

Lila's aunt Deirdre and her husband, Dwight.

Her cousins AnnaBeth, Jonas and Hunter. Myra and Cliff.

He didn't even mind when Miss ErmaJean and Miss GeorgeAnne arrived together. The Blue Ridge matchmakers had been in on this from the beginning. It was only fair they were present for the Christmas Eve culmination.

Everyone assembled on the porch.

"Thanks, everyone, for coming so quickly."

Miss ErmaJean clasped her gloves under her double chin. "We wouldn't miss it for the world."

"We reckoned you could use all the help you could get." Miss GeorgeAnne smirked.

She wasn't wrong.

"Did everybody bring warm coats, mittens and scarves?" IdaLee surveyed her troops. "You all understand your instructions?"

Heads bobbed.

This was either going to be the best night of his life. Or—he winced—the most humiliating. But either way, a Christmas Eve to remember.

His mother, Phil and Emma Cate were the last to arrive. Meeting them on the sidewalk, he crouched beside his daughter.

"Emma Cate, Mawmaw told you about why everyone is here tonight, right?"

Her blue eyes shone. "Dis is so exciting, Daddy."

But he had a moment of panic. If Lila didn't respond as he hoped, Emma Cate would be crushed. Maybe he should have asked his mom to wait at home with her until he knew for sure.

He chewed his lip. "Just so you know, Miss Penry may not say yes."

"Silly Daddy." Emma Cate placed her pink-gloved hands on his cheeks. "Of course Miss Penry will marry us. She doesn't think your face is too bristly at all."

Chuckling, his mother reached for Emma Cate's hand. He wished he felt as confident as his daughter.

God, forgive me for being stupid. Please let her still love me.

The sun began its descent. Clouds had gathered again. Truelove was probably in for more snow tonight. From every house up and down the street, lights glowed like candles in the windows.

It was go time.

The walk across the lawn had never felt as long. With every step, he was well aware of the eyes on his back. Monitoring his every move.

When he reached Lila's porch, he texted her that he was outside and would like to talk to her.

He waited a sec, but no little gray bubbles popped up. No reply. Which wasn't entirely unexpected. Or undeserved.

And the apple-green door remained closed.

This wasn't good. How was he going to propose if he couldn't get her to talk to him?

But if he was easily deterred, he never would've led the team to four conference titles. And with Lila, a more drastic action was obviously required.

He clomped up the steps and banged on the door. "Lila!" he shouted. "I know you're in there."

Silence, but she switched on the lights in her window.

He banged again. "I really need to talk to you. Please?" He banged again.

For good measure, he rang the doorbell. And continued to press the bell. In sporadic bursts.

She flung open the door. "For the love of Monet," she yelled. "Stop."

He took his finger off the buzzer.

She folded her arms across her sweater. "What are you doing here?"

As always, the sight of her made his heart speed up a little.

"I—I wanted to talk."

"What's there to say?" She pursed her lovely lips. "I think you made yourself perfectly clear."

There was a dangerous gleam in her eye, warning rapids ahead. Proceed with caution.

He'd known a few other people in his life with red on their head. Ordinarily possessing the mildest of dispositions, but once riled...

"Please forgive me. I didn't mean those things I said to you. You're nothing like Courtney."

She unfolded. "Was that everything you wanted to say to me?"

"I love you, Lila." His heart thundered. "Kind of desperately."

"Desperately?" A corner of her mouth lifted. "I love you, too, Sam."

Suddenly, he could breathe again. It was going to be okay. They were—

A dog barked on the street behind him. Her eyes narrowed. Glancing around him, she seemed to notice for the first time that they weren't alone.

"Mrs. Desmond? Mr. Thompson?" She angled toward IdaLee's house and gasped. "Dad. Mom. Emma Cate?" Her voice rose.

He turned in time to see his daughter wave. Their friends and family stood in Lila's driveway offering their support.

"Why are all these people here, Sam?"

"Because I want the whole world to know how wonderful I think you are." He got down on one knee.

Lila's eyes enlarged. Her hand flew to her throat.

"Emma Cate and I are so glad you've decided to stay in Truelove. We want to be a part of your life if you will allow us. Would you mar—"

"No." She held up her palm. "Wait."

There was a collective intake of breath behind him.

* * *

His to-die-for blue eyes bulged. His mouth opened and closed.

She wagged her finger. "Don't move."

Nodding mutely, he wobbled on his knee.

"Hang on." She turned on her heel. "I'll be right back," she called over her shoulder.

Racing into the house, she headed straight for her purse on the island in the kitchen. Heart pounding, she upended the contents of the bag on the counter. Searching. Scrabbling through the detritus of her life.

Aha! Found you.

Grabbing it, she raced outside. Half afraid he might have gone, but he hadn't. Everyone was exactly where she left them.

"Okay." She jogged back to the spot where she'd left him hanging. "Now where were we?"

He gaped at her.

"Oh yes. You are far from nothing, Samuel Gibson. I love you. You are everything I've ever wanted."

A vein pulsed in the exposed hollow of his throat above his open collar.

"But I know how you feel about getting something for nothing. So if it will make it easier for you, I propose we make a swap."

A sweet light entered his eyes. "What kind of swap?"

Smiling, she whipped out the green rubber band. "You're going to give me this. And in return, I'm going to spend the rest of my life loving you."

His Adam's apple bobbed. "You didn't throw it away."

"Did I mention how much I really, really love you, Sam Gibson?"

"Once or twice, and please don't ever stop."

She handed him the rubber hand.

When he looked at her like that, her heart wanted to beat right out of her chest.

Then it was like everything and everyone but the two of them faded away.

She smiled. "I think I might could arrange that."

He squared his shoulders. "Lila Pat Penry, will do you me the honor of becoming my wife? Of becoming Emma Cate's mom?"

Tears brimming in her eyes, she held out her hand. "Why, yes. Thank you. I'd be delighted to."

He placed the green rubber band on the third finger of her left hand. Twining his fingers through hers, he gave her a knee-buckling, ridiculously stomach-quivering smile.

Setting butterflies, dolphins and ponies prancing in her belly. He really did have the most debilitating effect on her nerve endings.

"Kiss her, Daddy!" Emma Cate shouted.

So he did.

Then everyone came up on the porch. Lots of hugs and well-wishes followed. Emma Cate gave Lila a picture she'd drawn of three figures standing in front of a reasonably accurate depiction of the little yellow house.

"Dat's Daddy." She pointed to the tallest figure in the drawing. "Dere's me and dere's…"

Lila smiled at the medium-height figure. Shoulder-length red curls. Big gray-blue eyes. And an absolutely fabulous fluttery scarf.

"—and you."

Lila hugged the small girl close. "I will cherish this forever. In fact . . ." She smiled. "I think we should frame it and mount on the wall so we can see it every day."

Soon after, the Christmas Eve revelers adjourned next door to the warmth of IdaLee's Victorian. But Lila and Sam lingered for a few moments at the bungalow.

"I'll need to call the bank." He glanced after Emma Cate, the drawing clutched in her mitten for safe-keeping. "Team Gibry, right?" He winked.

Her mouth quirked. "We'll work something out. No worries." She fluttered her hand. "But the most wonderful thing is that soon this will be the Gibson family home."

Catching her hand, he kissed her fingers. "The house where love lives."

"Team Gibson." She kissed his bristly cheek. "I think the real reason you want to marry me is because you love my house." She nudged him with her shoulder to let him know she was kidding.

He smirked. "It does have a fabulous paint job."

"Absolutely fabulous," she agreed.

He gave her a slow, crooked smile. "But no, my darlin' Lila."

The dragged-out drawl when he said her name caused goose bumps to rise and tingle on her skin like ladybugs dancing on her arms.

Sam pressed his forehead against hers. Beneath her palms, through the fabric of his shirt, she felt the steady rise and fall of his chest.

"I'm marrying you…" Smiling, he cradled the crown of her head, plowing and sifting his fingers in the heavy mass of her curls. "Because I love your hair."

* * * * *

If you enjoyed this story,
check out these other books
from author Lisa Carter

His Secret Daughter
The Twin Bargain
Stranded for the Holidays
A Mother's Homecoming

Find these and other great reads at
www.LoveInspired.com

Dear Reader,

The heart of this story is about learning to believe what God says about us.

Lila believed lies and didn't see herself as God saw her. Sam believed false things about himself, too. This wrong view of himself almost cost him the love, home and family he'd always dreamed of.

All too often, I've believed lies about myself instead of believing the truth of what God says about me. But God never lies. He loves me. He is faithful. And, dear reader, God is so very, very good.

The lies of the enemy seek only to steal our joy, to rob us of our hope for the future and to destroy the truth about who we are in Christ Jesus.

I pray that you and I will no longer give place to the lies we have believed about ourselves. But that we will see ourselves as God sees us—as His beloved, precious children.

May we always live in light of the happily-ever-after for which we're truly made.

I hope you enjoyed taking this journey with Lila, Sam and Emma Cate. I would love to hear from you. Email me at lisa@lisacarterauthor.com or visit www.lisacarterauthor.com.

In His love,
Lisa Carter

Get 4 FREE REWARDS!

We'll send you 2 FREE Books plus 2 FREE Mystery Gifts.

Love Inspired Suspense books showcase how courage and optimism unite in stories of faith and love in the face of danger.

FREE Value Over $20

YES! Please send me 2 FREE Love Inspired Suspense novels and my 2 FREE mystery gifts (gifts are worth about $10 retail). After receiving them, if I don't wish to receive any more books, I can return the shipping statement marked "cancel." If I don't cancel, I will receive 6 brand-new novels every month and be billed just $5.24 each for the regular-print edition or $5.99 each for the larger-print edition in the U.S., or $5.74 each for the regular-print edition or $6.24 each for the larger-print edition in Canada. That's a savings of at least 13% off the cover price. It's quite a bargain! Shipping and handling is just 50¢ per book in the U.S. and $1.25 per book in Canada.* I understand that accepting the 2 free books and gifts places me under no obligation to buy anything. I can always return a shipment and cancel at any time. The free books and gifts are mine to keep no matter what I decide.

Choose one: ☐ **Love Inspired Suspense Regular-Print** (153/353 IDN GNWN) ☐ **Love Inspired Suspense Larger-Print** (107/307 IDN GNWN)

Name (please print)

Address   Apt. #

City   State/Province   Zip/Postal Code

Email: Please check this box ☐ if you would like to receive newsletters and promotional emails from Harlequin Enterprises ULC and its affiliates. You can unsubscribe anytime.

Mail to the **Reader Service:**
IN U.S.A.: P.O. Box 1341, Buffalo, NY 14240-8531
IN CANADA: P.O. Box 603, Fort Erie, Ontario L2A 5X3

Want to try 2 free books from another series? Call 1-800-873-8635 or visit www.ReaderService.com.

---

*Terms and prices subject to change without notice. Prices do not include sales taxes, which will be charged (if applicable) based on your state or country of residence. Canadian residents will be charged applicable taxes. Offer not valid in Quebec. This offer is limited to one order per household. Books received may not be as shown. Not valid for current subscribers to Love Inspired Suspense books. All orders subject to approval. Credit or debit balances in a customer's account(s) may be offset by any other outstanding balance owed by or to the customer. Please allow 4 to 6 weeks for delivery. Offer available while quantities last.

Your Privacy—Your information is being collected by Harlequin Enterprises ULC, operating as Reader Service. For a complete summary of the information we collect, how we use this information and to whom it is disclosed, please visit our privacy notice located at corporate.harlequin.com/privacy-notice. From time to time we may also exchange your personal information with reputable third parties. If you wish to opt out of this sharing of your personal information, please visit readerservice.com/consumerschoice or call 1-800-873-8635. **Notice to California Residents**—Under California law, you have specific rights to control and access your data. For more information on these rights and how to exercise them, visit corporate.harlequin.com/california-privacy.

LIS20R2